WITCH AT HEART

The Jinx Hamilton Series - Book 1

JULIETTE HARPER

Chapter One

You've heard that old saying, "Be careful what you ask for, little girl, you may get it." Well, I am living proof that, sometimes, old saws can be cutting edge. I said all I wanted to do was work at home and have as many cats as I could afford. Maybe it was wish fulfillment or karma smacking me in the backside, but I am now single, 29, and the unpaid servant to four well-fed felines. We all live in the apartment above the store that I inherited from my Crazy Aunt Fiona. No. Seriously. That's what we called her. Crazy Aunt Fiona.

I can see my mother now, handing me the kitchen telephone receiver, the one with the cord stretched out so straight you could wander over half the house. "Norma Jean, get in here and talk to your Crazy Aunt Fiona."

Yes, you read that right. Norma Jean. Mom loves Marilyn Monroe and chose to punish me with her obsession. Thank God Daddy heard that and said, "Lord God, woman, you have jinxed this child for life." That's the name that stuck. Jinx. Most people don't even know my real name.

Mine was a pretty conventional Southern Baptist raising in our tiny town. Mom is the devout one. Dad and I concentrate on staying out of trouble. By the time I made it to high school, I understood that we were actually "dancing Baptists." Come Sunday morning, a certain brand of amnesia kicks in about where the family might have been the night before and how much country music could have been involved in the activity.

Crazy Aunt Fiona lived one town over and ran what mom referred to as a "rat's nest of a tourist trap." I could never figure out the second part of that statement since there wasn't much in our neck of the woods to see. That was before I understood that some people live all their lives cooped up in cities and can't wait to enjoy some real countryside.

The other part, about the rat's nest, was a no-brainer. Dad swore a guy could walk in off the street and say, "Excuse me, do you have a spark plug for a Studebaker?" and Fiona'd have one. She sold everything from penny candy at the counter to love potions out the back door. You want a MoonPie and some fishing worms? Fiona had it.

The idea of a coherent inventory or any particular purpose for her store never seemed to enter her mind. When she decided she wanted to serve food, the health board got all bent out of shape. Fiona happily took the required state course, met their standards for food preparation, and went on about her business—as long as the food inspector wasn't in sight.

"Everybody that comes in this place drinks homemade whiskey and would cook roadkill if it looked fresh enough," Fiona declared. "They're not gonna be catching bubonic plague germs from me."

Truth be told, lots of folks came to Fiona to heal from whatever ailed them at the time. One summer, I was sitting on the stool behind the counter when a woman came in who had just buried her husband. She and Fiona stepped off to one side, and I heard the woman say, "Mrs. Ryan, my heart hurts so bad without Jesse, I can't breathe."

Aunt Fiona disappeared into the storeroom and came back

with a piece of rose quartz on a silver chain. She said, "Now, honey, you wear this over your heart so the magic can help you start healing. You get to thinking you can't breathe, you hold onto this piece of quartz and you pray to Jesus."

After the woman left, I said, "Aunt Fiona, how can a rock make that lady feel better about her dead husband?"

Aunt Fiona reached over and tucked my long hair behind my ears and patted my cheek with her ring-bedecked, blue-veined hand. "It's not the rock that will heal her honey, it's the belief that she *can* heal."

Aunt Fiona expressed deep, wise ideas that were also simple and loving. People called Aunt Fiona a witch woman, but the only spells I ever saw her cast were good common sense and a lot of love.

When she passed on, I was still working the same job I got the week after I graduated high school—waiting tables down at Tom's Cafe. It wasn't a bad job. I made enough to feed my cats first, and then myself with what was left over. I saw everybody in town every day, and the men only made half-hearted passes at me for the fun of it. Nobody really tried to hassle me.

The longer I worked there and the more cats I collected, the more mom clucked and said I would wind up a "touched," old spinster like Aunt Fiona. Then Fiona died. Judge Baker called me into his office where I learned my aunt left me the shop and a nice sum of money.

My mother had a fit, but I moved myself and my cats to Briar Hollow. I figured once I got there, I'd learn how to run the place. If I kept stocking the same stuff Aunt Fiona put out and people kept buying it, I should be at least mildly successful. My basic plan was to fake running the store until I really knew how to do it and could make the business my own.

That first day when I pushed the wilted funeral wreath aside and turned the old skeleton key in the lock, the smell of lemon verbena that always lingered in the store made my throat close. At my feet, my cats, Zeke, Yule, Xavier, and Winston yowled to be let out of their carriers. (I decided to start at the end of the alphabet and work backward. If I get another one, he'll be Vernon.)

All my cats are toms. Big lovable couch potatoes who purr just because you walk in the room. They're strictly inside cats and prefer good air conditioning. It was early spring, but I did not want to listen to the boys complain once summer set in. Replacing Aunt Fiona's old swamp cooler topped my upgrade list.

I took the carriers upstairs and blessed Aunt Fiona for her double entry system. The stairs at the back of the store led to a door that opened on a small vestibule. The next door put you in the apartment proper. Both could be locked, to prevent any unplanned escapes, not that my guys could summon up that much energy anyway.

As soon as I opened the carriers, the gang set out to investigate their new digs. I shut the door behind me and went back down for my suitcase. The boxes could wait until morning. When I looked up at the storefront from the street, a pair of cats sat in each of the big windows animatedly discussing their view of downtown Briar Hollow.

Lots of people might balk at the idea of living above a store on the town's Main Street, but Briar Hollow is a sleepy burg on the edge of the Blue Ridge. We get our fair share of summer tourists, and even more come leaf season, but I doubted there would be any need to phone the sheriff's office with noise complaints. The dispatcher would be hard-pressed to wake up long enough to take the call anyway.

Aunt Fiona's store—well, my store now—sits across the street from the courthouse. My front windows look straight at the Confederate Veterans' monument, complete with cannon and cannonballs. We like to tell the Yankees we're over the War of Northern Aggression. God knows their tourist dollars spend just fine. Truth be told, I'm betting the local Sons of the Confederacy keep that piece of artillery in firing condition.

Next door on the right, Amity Prescott runs a local craft shop complete with art classes. When I came over for Aunt Fiona's funeral, Amity told me I *had* to keep the store open on Wednesday nights from now on. "That's when I host the 'Draw Pictures While Drinking Wine' evenings," Amity said. "By the third bottle, they all think they're Picasso, and they'll buy damned near anything."

On the left, Chase McGregor has his cobbler's shop. He repairs footwear and makes custom leather goods, everything from journal covers to boots for Civil War reenactors. The smell of new leather wafts out his front door, and well, to be honest, Chase is not hard on the eyes—and he's a fellow cat lover. His cat, a lame ginger named Festus, never limps farther than the bench by the front door. He spends his mornings taking the sun and greeting passersby.

If the *Travel Channel* ever bothered to show up in town, they'd label Briar Hollow "bucolic and bohemian." For me, being here is a chance for something more in life than waiting on tables. I love Aunt Fiona even more for thinking enough of me to leave me her shop.

That first night, I settled in her big brass bed with all four of my cats and stared out the window at the moon rising over the courthouse. Just before sleep claimed me, I remember saying, "Aunt Fiona, if you were a witch, I hope you left me your magic, too."

That might have been where I made my mistake.

Chapter Two

The next morning, a little after dawn, I woke up under the combined and forceful gaze of four cats used to being fed at 5:00 a.m.

"Come on," I groused. "We talked about this. There is no breakfast shift. The store opens at nine. You all can wait."

The cats exchanged a communal look of resignation. Clearly, they didn't want to have to do this the hard way, but I left them no choice, and, after a silent vote, Winston drew the short straw. He shook his head as if to say, "It didn't have to come to this," right before he jumped off the bed. In seconds, he reappeared on the dresser and lifted his paw in the direction of a porcelain figurine, a 19th century lady in a bonnet complete with a bouquet of flowers.

"You wouldn't!" I said, outraged.

Winston nudged the knickknack toward the edge and looked at me. In the crowd at the foot of the bed, three heads swiveled toward me. It was my turn in this contest of wills.

"Winston," I said sternly, "you get down from there right now."

That was not only a useless statement; it was a serious breach of etiquette. Cats don't like to be ordered around.

Winston fixed me with a sorrowful expression and that line from *The Godfather* shot across my mind. *It's just business.* As I watched, he scooted the delicate object to the lip of the dresser and looked at me without blinking. A long moment passed. I refused to be the one to break. Not again. Not this time. No sir . . .

Fur met porcelain.

I cracked.

Throwing back the covers in a panic, I exclaimed, "Okay, *fine*," but it was too late.

The breakable flower lady teetered and fell. My hand shot out even though I was too far away to catch the fragile object. As I watched, the figurine slowed and hung suspended in mid-air.

Without really knowing why, I brought my hand up, lifting the lady with it. When the endangered kitsch was once again level with the top of the dresser, I pushed forward gently and watched as it settled safely in place.

Winston observed the whole process with studied feline impassiveness. Once the figurine landed, he sniffed it and gave me an imperceptible nod. *Well played, human.* Then he jumped down, and the entire pack went into the kitchen. All they wanted was for me to get up and feed them; they really didn't care how that was accomplished.

As for me, I stood rooted in place, my mouth hanging open waiting for a fly to go buzzing right on in. I don't know how long I would have stayed frozen there if the boys hadn't started raising the roof with their yowling.

I shuffled into the kitchen, flipped the light on, and doled out the morning rations. With a line of dining cats at my feet, I shook my head. "Get a grip, Jinx," I said aloud. "That was nothing but a half-awake dream. Serves you right for eating *Doritos* at bedtime."

Xavier looked up at me telegraphing his agreement. He's a *Cheetos* man.

Talking to yourself qualifies as a major perk of living with cats. If anyone comes in the room, you blame it all on the fur balls. "It *must* have been a dream," I continued, stubbornly reasoning with myself. "That's what happens when you spoiled brats wake me up out of a sound sleep. Everyone knows you can't put out your hand like that and . . ."

All the cats looked up when my self-justifying monologue morphed into a choking gurgle that sounded like a hairball on its way north.

I'm one of those people who can't talk if her hands are tied behind her back. When I said the words "put out your hand," I went through the motion, accidentally raising a loaf of *Wonder Bread* clean off the counter where it now floated suspended in air beside the spice rack.

Cautiously, I drew my outstretched hand toward my body, and the bread followed. As it crossed the room, Zeke jumped and made a grab for the plastic wrapper. On instinct, I jerked like I was pulling on a rope and the *Wonder Bread* shot at me like a guided missile, thwacking me in the face before landing at my feet, scattering cats right and left.

Curious to see if it would work, I crooked my index finger toward the loaf, using the classic "come here" motion. The bread obeyed like a well-trained coonhound.

Standing there with the *Wonder Bread* in my hand, I asked the cats, "You all saw that, right?"

A voice behind me answered. "They saw it, and so did I, honey."

It was my turn to jump like I'd been shot. When I whirled around, ready to beat off some attacker armed with nothing but a loaf of white bread, I found Aunt Fiona standing in the doorway leading out to the living room.

"Hi, Jinx," she said pleasantly, before adding with a hint of concern, "I think maybe you better sit down before you fall down, sugar."

"No," I said, starting to back up. "Not only no, but hell no. I am not going to be seeing dead people."

"You're not seeing just *any* dead people, Jinx," Aunt Fiona said soothingly. "I'm your kin."

By this time, my back had hit the refrigerator, and I had no choice but to stop. When I didn't say anything, Aunt Fiona went on. "You're squishing that bread, honey. Put it down."

My mother raised me to mind my elders, so I did as I was told, staring at Aunt Fiona all the while. My deceased aunt couldn't have looked more like herself. Her long, gray hair was tied back, and she wore her usual "uniform"—baggy jeans and a loose peasant blouse—which was odd since we buried her in a pink polyester pantsuit.

When I said as much, Fiona actually glared at me. "That's a bone that needs picking with you, Jinx Hamilton. Why in tarnation did you let your Mama put me in that God-awful git up?"

Like I had any control over what my mother got in her head was "fitting and proper."

Setting my own mouth in a firm line, I said, "And just how was I going to stop her?"

Aunt Fiona let out a disgruntled "harrumph," which I took as a sign of begrudging agreement. My mother was her baby sister, the last of nine children, and, according to Fiona, Mom couldn't help it that she had a stick up her . . . well, you get the idea.

This was not happening. I needed to hit the reset button on this whole thing.

Without saying a word to my Aunt Fiona, who simply *could*

not be there, I marched myself downstairs in my pajamas, stepped out onto the sidewalk, took several deep breaths, and said, "Okay. Now. You're awake. That was a dream. Go back up there and start this day over."

Just then a man walked by and gave me an odd look.

I wished him a good morning and then caught sight of myself in the front window of the store. I was wearing pink bunny slippers, and my pajamas were covered in unicorns and rainbows. Okay then. Crazy lady on Main Street. Great. Just great.

Sheepishly, I went back inside, climbed the stairs, walked into the kitchen, and there sat Aunt Fiona.

No more beating around the bush. I looked Fiona right in the eye and said, "Aren't you supposed to 'go into the light' or something like that once you're dead?"

Aunt Fiona sighed. "You've seen too many movies, honey. Have you had your coffee?"

"No, ma'am."

"Well, make yourself a cup," Aunt Fiona ordered. "You know you can't think straight without some caffeine in your system. Use that fancy coffee maker of mine. The little 'k-thingies' are in the cupboard up there on the left."

Still, on obedient autopilot, I made my coffee and joined Aunt Fiona, who had installed herself at the kitchen table. I didn't realize ghosts used furniture, but there she sat, dangling a little piece of string for Yule, who was swatting at it happily.

"The cats can see you, too?" I asked, sitting down warily.

"Animals are a lot smarter than humans," Fiona said. "I thought you knew that already." She let Yule steal the string and turned her full attention to me as he galloped off into the front room. "So, do you like the apartment?"

"Aunt Fiona," I said, "I *have* been here before."

"I know, honey, but it's yours now," she said, looking around wistfully as if she missed the place already. "Now, don't you go being sentimental about my stuff," she added. "Throw it all out if you want to. This is your home now."

I had the good manners to say "thank you" before blurting out, "What the heck is going on, Aunt Fiona?"

She regarded me with surprise. "Just exactly what you asked for."

"What I asked for?" I said, dumbfounded. "What exactly did I ask for?"

"Before you went to sleep last night, you asked me to give you my magic," she said brightly. "So I did."

The words were hardly out of her mouth before I put both hands in front of my face trying to ward off the words.

"No, no, no, no, no," I chanted adamantly. "That's not what I meant. Not at all. No. Really. Thank you but take it back. Please."

Aunt Fiona's smile wilted at the edges. "But, honey," she said, "I can't. Once your powers wake up, they're yours for life. It's not like returning something at *Sears & Roebuck*."

I couldn't believe what I was hearing. "You're kidding me, right?" I finally asked weakly.

"Jinx," she scolded, "I would never joke with you about something this important."

Letting that sink in for a minute, and with no small degree of trepidation, I tried to get more information. "Why am I just hearing about this witch thing now?"

"Because you wouldn't have believed it before," Aunt Fiona said. "You can be rather . . . literal, dear."

I mulled that over and grudgingly had to admit Fiona was right.

While I wasn't exactly ready to *believe* the witch thing now, something was clearly going on. "Okay," I said, taking a deep breath, "what exactly are these so-called 'powers' anyway?"

"I have no idea," Fiona said with happy enthusiasm. "You can certainly use telekinesis; that's moving things with your mind. And you can see me, which means you should be able to see other spirits, but from there, your powers will be what you make of them. They'll come a little bit at a time according to what's right for you. I remember when it happened to me, it was like getting a surprise birthday present every day. You'll love it."

That I doubted seriously. "Look, Aunt Fiona, I really appreciate the, uh, thought, but even if you can't take these powers back, I'm not going to use them."

Aunt Fiona seemed to be struggling to find a diplomatic way to say what came out next. "They don't like to be ignored, Jinx," she said finally. "Trying to stifle your powers won't work out the way you think it will."

This was really getting to be too much. I stood up and started pacing back and forth in the kitchen—jabbering without any real thought about what was coming out of my mouth. "I am not going to have this," I said. "I'm the only person who runs my own life. Just because somebody gives you a gift doesn't mean you have to use it or like it or . . ."

"Jinx," Aunt Fiona said sternly. "Stop! You're making me dizzy."

I stopped, took a breath, and plopped down in the chair. There had to be a way out of this, I thought as I concentrated on not hyperventilating because passing out didn't seem like a good option at the moment. Lord only knows what I'd find when I came to.

Neither one of us said anything for a minute, and from the expression on Aunt Fiona's face, I realized I might be stuck being a . . . witch. That idea left me feeling dizzy myself. I looked at my aunt and said, imploringly, "But you'll be here to help me, right?"

Aunt Fiona leaned over and put her hands on my face—or at least it felt like she did because I wasn't exactly sure a ghost could touch someone. Her eyes met mine and she said, "Jinx, ever since you were a little girl, you've always known what was right in your heart. You're going to figure this all out. If I didn't know that in *my* heart, I never would have given you the powers in the first place. You just be you and everything will be fine."

With that, she stood up to leave.

"Wait!" I cried, suddenly panic-stricken. "You're not leaving, are you? You can't leave! You have to stay here and tell me what to do next."

"Oh, don't be silly," Fiona answered crisply as if admonishing me to go forth and do battle. "I have a brand-new afterlife to lead. You'll catch on fast. I'll try to pop in and check on you from time to time, but I have no idea what my schedule will be like."

Schedule? Dead people have schedules? Before I could ask what in the world she would be doing, Aunt Fiona started to fade out right in front of me. "Hey!" I cried. "Wait a minute! Really! You can't go."

"Sorry, honey," Fiona said, her voice growing more distant. "I have to run. I just wanted to check in and congratulate you on getting your magic. Enjoy running the store. Sorry I left things in a bit of a mess. Oh, and there's a very nice rat in the storeroom. His name is Rodney. Now, don't you dare hurt him. He only takes what he needs."

Seriously? All of this, *and* I get saddled with a rodent named Rodney?

"Aunt Fiona . . ."

But it was no use. She was gone.

New superpowers. A ghost. And a resident rat. All before six o'clock in the morning. Go me.

Chapter Three

So that's how my new life got started. I *really* wasn't ready to embrace the idea of being some kind of witch, no matter what Aunt Fiona said. In truth, I needed to put the idea completely out of my mind. I figured the best option was to get to work in the store and put off the complicated thinking for later. The cats were all settled in on the sofa sound asleep. I closed both doors tight behind me and went downstairs.

Beyond the fact that I didn't want the boys getting out, I also didn't relish the thought of them finding Rodney the Rat. Aunt Fiona said he lived in the storeroom. If we were going to be roomies, introductions were in order. Gingerly reaching around the doorframe, I clicked on the light and said, hesitantly, "Hey, Rodney. You around?"

A rustling noise answered my question. A pink nose flanked by luxuriant, white whiskers peeked out between two ridiculously large cans of horse liniment. When Fiona said rat, I was expecting a four-legged street thug with a file tail and an eye patch. Instead, I was looking at a black and white domesticated rat that must have decided to strike out on his own. Intelligence gleamed in the dark eyes, and he showed no fear at my presence.

"Well," I said, "look at you, all handsome and everything. Are we going to be friends?"

The rat's nose twitched, and he stepped further into the light, eyeing me expectantly. I saw a tin of crackers on the small worktable. I opened it and offered Rodney a saltine. He politely reached out with paws, as agile as any human hands, and delicately accepted the gift. I continued to study him as he munched away. One cracker, and the little guy stole my heart.

When he finished, I asked, "Where do you live?"

Rodney turned around and started back in the shadows, but paused and looked over his shoulder as if beckoning me to follow. Cautiously I pushed the two cans aside and discovered a tidy cage complete with a running wheel and nest box. The water bottle hanging from the bars was almost empty.

"I'm sorry, Rodney," I said, unclipping the bottle. "Aunt Fiona just now told me about you." As I carried the bottle to the deep utility sink on the far side of the room, I felt the rat's eyes on me. When I returned and installed his fresh water supply, he stood up on his hind legs and rested his front paws on the edge of my hand. The message was clear. I would do.

"Pleased to meet you, too," I said softly. "I have to go to work now, but I'll come clean out your room later. Okay?"

Rodney seemed to be in perfect agreement. He ambled back to his bachelor pad and made straight for the nest box, apparently intent on taking a nap.

The rat turned out to be the best part of the morning.

Although I had long been aware of Aunt Fiona's spontaneous approach to stocking her shelves, I never guessed how eclectic her inventory really was until I began to go through it all.

I surmised that the business began as a general mercantile store. Fiona added herbs, soaps, and essential oils, along with odd detritus supporting those products. Then, out of nowhere, I dragged out a brand-new sausage grinder in a dusty, unopened box.

For a minute I panicked. What was I going to do if someone walked in the door and asked me to find something? Then it dawned on me. I'm the boss. I didn't have to open for business. Rummaging around until I found a black marker, I carefully lettered a sign on a piece of cardboard and taped it to the front door.

"Closed for Inventory."

It might as well have said, "Closed for Dumpster Diving."

Surveying the retail jigsaw puzzle and refusing to be defeated, I opted for a thematic approach based on the sausage grinder. Hardware first.

For two hours, I crawled under tables. I survived precariously balancing on a ladder. In the end, I amassed a haphazard pile of items near the foot of the stairs:

- the sausage grinder
- fifteen sets of jumper cables
- assorted copper fittings
- six green garden hoses
- various cans of paint in lurid colors
- countless boxes of nuts, bolts, screws, and nails

All of that came from the left side of the center "aisle" that more or less divided the store.

In the process of "categorizing" that heap, I also found a hookah pipe, four Ouija boards, an inflatable Frosty the Snowman, and a complete set of Encyclopedia Britannica from 1957.

I needed help.

The lighted refrigerator behind the counter hummed and emitted a blast of cold air when I opened the door. I took out a soda and twisted off the cap, taking a long pull of carbonated goodness. There were some sandwiches in triangle-shaped plastic boxes on the top shelf. Squinting at the expiration dates, I decided all of them were well within non-lethal range. I pulled the plastic back from a ham and cheese on white, plopped down on the tall stool behind the cash register, and chewed contemplatively.

Aunt Fiona made the store work by the sheer force of her personality and what appeared to be a memory that would put an elephant to shame. Until I cultivated my own "presence" as a shopkeeper, I needed a better plan than faking it. Surely there was a way to both preserve the "eclectic emporium" vibe *and* come up with a more coherent selling point to bring people in the door.

The fact that Fiona had drinks and snacks was good. I could ace the state test, so going for an old-fashioned soda counter wasn't a bad idea. I found a yellowed pad of paper on a shelf under the cash register along with a stubby pencil. It was time to make a list.

I wrote "Store Ideas" on the top of the sheet, drew a line under it, and then penciled, "soda fountain." The herbs and essential oils scattered around on random shelves were all in great shape and should sell well, especially if I brought in some nice soaps and maybe some natural scents. Aunt Fiona stocked an astonishing array of crystals, some loose and others set in jewelry. Lots of people believe those things have powers . . .

My mind flashed back to the day Aunt Fiona gave that grieving widow the rose quartz. Oh my God. What if that necklace really did have some kind of power attached? Was all this mess a cover for a magic shop? Were the people who came in here going to expect me to do the things for them Aunt Fiona did? What the *heck* did Aunt Fiona do?

My heart raced. I didn't just need help, I needed somebody

to talk to who wouldn't freak out when I announced, "Hey, by the way, I'm a witch."

I dug my phone out of the back pocket of my jeans and speed dialed my best friend, Tori. She answered on the fourth ring. "Have you lost your mind?" she hissed by way of greeting. "If Tom catches me on the phone during the lunch hour, he's gonna pitch a fit."

I glanced at the clock and winced. "Sorry, I didn't look at the time. Isn't this your weekend off?"

"Yeah," she said. "I'm a free woman come five o'clock."

"Want to spend it with me and the boys?" I asked hopefully.

Tori must have heard the strain in my voice. "Are you okay, Jinksy?" she asked.

Nobody but Tori calls me Jinksy.

"I don't know," I admitted. "There's some weird stuff going on over here."

In the background, I heard Tom bellow, "Tori! Order up!"

"I gotta go," Tori said. "I'll throw some stuff in a bag and drive over after work." She started to end the call and then said, "Whatever's going on, Jinksy, we'll figure it out like we always do. Okay?"

"Okay," I answered, relief flooding my system. Tori always had my back.

The two of us had been "figuring stuff out" since our moms brought us home from the hospital three days apart, plunked us down on the floor together, and declared that we would be best friends.

My mom, Kelly, is into Marilyn Monroe, and Tori's mom, Gemma, has a thing for Tallulah Bankhead. They were BFFs, emphasis on the "forever" part, and it never occurred to them that Tori and I wouldn't carry on the tradition. The moms raised us like sisters, but I think that's how Tori and I would have felt about each other anyway.

Everybody needs that one friend who "gets" them. If I had called Tori and said, "Bring a shovel," she wouldn't have asked if we were planting roses or burying a no-good boyfriend, she'd just show up ready to dig.

Since Tori couldn't possibly make it to the store earlier than six o'clock, I decided to walk down to the corner grocery and get a few things for the weekend. Snacks were in order—as in chocolate and wine. I went upstairs and put out fresh dry food for the cats. They had already staked out their observation posts of choice in the front windows. In a few days, they'd know the routine on Main Street like the fur on their own paws.

When I came in the night before, I tossed my bag on the end table inside the door, but now my keys were nowhere to be found. "Damn it," I muttered, scanning the flat surfaces in the living room. I must have put the keys down in an absent-minded moment. I did that with my sunglasses once, and it took me three days to find them—in the dishwasher.

Zeke gave me an inquisitive "Meow?"

"I'm looking for my keys," I answered. "I don't want to waste time hunting for the darn things."

No sooner were the words out of my mouth than a merry jingling sounded from the top of the bookshelf by the fireplace. My keys danced toward me, sailing through the air with a happy rhythm that sounded vaguely like a bossa nova. (Dance class. Eight years. I know these things.)

The keys stopped, suspended in front of me at a convenient level, my lucky four-leaf clover keyring standing straight upright as if held in place by an invisible hand. Since I didn't know what else to do, I reached out and took hold of the keys, half-expecting to feel . . . something. I might as well have been lifting them off a nail on the wall.

Okay. I had to admit that was kind of . . .

"No," I said aloud. "Not cool. Not cool *at all*."

Four furry heads swiveled in protest as if to say, "We're not doing anything!"

"Not you guys," I clarified crossly. "No to magic. I am not using magic."

I was still chanting that refrain when I closed the second door and started down the stairs. Every time my foot hit a step I said "No to magic" under my breath.

Of course, there was one problem. Since I didn't know how I was doing any of these things in the first place, how was I going to stop doing them?

Chapter Four

When I stepped out on the sidewalk in front of the shop at about one o'clock, I discovered I had missed the better part of a glorious day digging through Aunt Fiona's inventory. No wonder the cats were glued to the front windows upstairs. Although the summer tourist season hadn't started, there were a fair number of people walking up and down Main Street. The grocery store sat at the far end of the block from the shop. I waved at Amity in the pottery studio as I walked by and paused for a minute to look at the clothes in the window of Aggie's Dress Emporium.

The bell on the door announced my arrival at George and Irma's Grocery and Dry Goods. The place was exactly as I remembered, from the sagging, well-worn wood floors to the vintage tin ceiling overhead.

George was on a ladder getting a box down, and Irma was behind the counter reading an historical romance. My mother reads the same kind of books. Think half-naked hunk with long hair on the cover and a plot set someplace swashbuckling in another century. This guy appeared to be wearing a kilt, so my guess was Scotland.

"Oh, Jinx!" Irma cried, putting the book down and coming out from behind the counter to give me a big, motherly hug. She had to stand on tiptoe to accomplish the maneuver. Irma was stretching it to make five feet.

George, a grandfatherly bear of a man who towered over his wife, lumbered down the ladder and put his arms around both of us. I wasn't expecting a group hug, but given how the day had gone so far, I didn't turn it down either.

"Are you all moved in, sugar?" Irma asked, still holding me at arm's length.

"You need any help carrying in boxes?" George chimed in, keeping a protective arm around each of us.

"Do you have enough food in the house?" Irma added earnestly, implying I faced imminent starvation.

I laughed, remembering how hard it was to get a word in edgewise when they were both being parental, which was most of the time.

"Hi, Irma. Hi, George," I said. "I drove over last night with my cats. I've already taken all my stuff upstairs but thank you. I am here to get a few groceries. My friend Tori is coming for the weekend."

"Oh, that's good, honey," Irma said. "I don't know what I would do without my girlfriends. We are so sorry about Fiona. My goodness, I can't imagine this block without her. The service was real nice, honey, and Fiona looked so . . . proper . . . in her casket."

"The pink pantsuit was mom's idea," I said grinning. "Aunt Fiona would have hated it, wouldn't she?"

George burst out laughing. "I'm surprised she's not already haunting you for putting her in that thing."

If he only knew.

"You look around and get whatever you need, honey," Irma said, stepping behind the counter. "Take your time. Oh, and be sure to tell me what kind of food and litter your kitties like. If we don't carry it, I'll get some for you."

Say what you want about life in small towns like Briar Hollow. For every nosy busybody spreading gossip, there are a dozen of good-hearted people with a genuine desire to help folks out.

I spent a few minutes going up and down the aisles getting the essentials which meant lots of chips, cookies, chocolate, and wine, as well as frozen mac n' cheese in case we needed real nutrition.

As I put the items on the counter for Irma to ring up, she said, "Do we need to keep filling all of Fiona's standing orders for you?"

Standing orders. What the heck did that mean?

"Well," I hedged, "I'm not sure. What kind of things did you all get for her?"

Irma reached under the counter and brought out an old-fashioned index card file box. She flipped through the cards and extracted one, studying it for a second before she handed it to me.

I accepted the card and looked at the list of items. Why in the world would Aunt Fiona need a weekly supply of something called wheatgrass? And I didn't even know if "nori" was a person or a thing.

"Uh, could we put all of this on hold until I figure out if these are items she actually used in the store?"

"Of course," Irma said. "You decide what you need, and we'll find a way to get it even if it's something that's hard to come by."

I didn't tell her that Amazon took care of most of my exotic shopping problems, but I wasn't sure even the massive online retailer could tackle Aunt Fiona's list.

My ordinary comfort food purchases fit easily in two bags. When I returned to the shop, Festus, the lame resident cat from next door, was sunning himself on the bench under the front window. I put my bags down and went over to talk to him. Festus and I were old friends, so when I sat down and scratched his ginger ears, he began to purr like a jet engine.

I was so engrossed in cooing over Festus, I didn't hear Chase McGregor come out of the leather shop. "Hi, Jinx," he said in a friendly voice. "You getting all settled in?"

When I looked up, my heart did its usual flutter at the sight of the man. Chase probably doesn't stand more than about six feet tall, but he's broad across the chest and well built. A long leather apron covered his plaid shirt and jeans. He was wiping his hands with a rag.

"Hi, Chase," I said, answering his greeting. "Sorry I talked to Festus first before sticking my head in to say hello."

"Oh, I'm used to it," he said, sitting down on the other side of the yellow cat. "Festus is a regular ladies' man. He always snags the pretty girls before I can talk to them."

Did he just lump me in the "pretty girl" category?

In spite of my best efforts, I felt a flush of pleasure rise in my cheeks. Recognizing my embarrassment, Chase smoothly continued the conversation.

Handsome *and* sweet.

"You stocking up on junk food?" he asked, gesturing toward my bags. Three different cookie packages poked out.

I laughed. "Yes, but it's not all for me," I said. "I'm overwhelmed by Aunt Fiona's inventory, so I asked my friend Tori to come over for the weekend and help out."

Chase shook his head. "I don't think you can go through all Fiona's stuff in one weekend."

"Oh, I don't think so either," I admitted. "I'm hoping we can come up with a plan and maybe get the store headed in a more definite direction."

"I completely understand," he said. "Fiona wasn't big on planning. She made things work by feel. I don't think that approach would work for anyone but her." He paused, and his voice broke on the next words. "I'm going to miss her," he said. "She was like my second mom."

"Thank you, Chase," I said sincerely. "That is so sweet. I know you meant a lot to Aunt Fiona, too."

His blue eyes met my green ones and there was no guile or ulterior motive in what he said next. "I want to be your friend, too, Jinx. Call me anytime you like. I live over my shop. Bang on the pipes in the corner of your kitchen, and I'll know to come over. That's the signal Fiona used."

"What did she call you to help with?" I asked curiously.

"Mainly opening stubborn lids and eating cookies warm out of the oven," he grinned.

I grinned back. "I'll remember that you have expertise in both areas."

"I'm well-versed in chocolate chip," he teased. "It's a particular area of specialization."

We both let the flirtatious moment hang enjoyably in the air for a minute and then I said, "Okay. I guess I better let you get back to work. Tori's going to be here around suppertime."

Although he agreed with me, Chase didn't look like he wanted to go back to work, or maybe I wanted to *think* he didn't look that way. As I bent down to retrieve my bags, he said, "Hey, tell you what. How about I bring some pizza over tomorrow for lunch? I'm only open half days on Saturday until tourist season gets going good. We all have to eat, and if you need any heavy lifting done, I can help you then."

Since I wanted to get to know Chase better and, Tori would have my head if I turned down an offer involving both food and a hunky guy, I accepted. "That would be great, but, please, don't go to any trouble."

"No trouble at all," he said happily. "There's a new place across the street that makes pizza in a wood-fired oven. They're fantastic. Any preferences?"

"As long as there are no anchovies involved, we're both open to anything."

"Perfect. How about one o'clock?"

We agreed and said our good-byes. As I closed the door, Chase picked Festus up. I heard him say, "Come on, old man. Time for your supper. I'll save you the walk."

Handsome. Kind. Cat lover. Is that hitting a triple or what?

Chapter Five

Going to the grocery store and visiting with Chase and Festus took up the better part of an hour and a half. Then my boys needed attention, so I didn't get back to work until after three o'clock. I made it halfway down the stairs before my heart sank. How would I tame the chaos, even with Tori's help?

"What am I supposed to do?" I said speaking directly to the shop. "Ask you to produce a butter mold and, presto, it appears?"

Let me give you a word of advice. When someone tells you that you're a witch, don't use words like "presto" and speak to possibly enchanted spaces unless you're prepared for the unexpected.

On a middle shelf to my right, a stack of cookbooks and a box of light bulbs obligingly moved aside. A butter mold in the shape of a rooster scooted to the front and slid into thin air. It executed a series of merry somersaults before stopping upside down a foot from me.

"You're standing on your head," I said sarcastically.

The butter mold flipped around and gave a bobble that looked for all the world like the rooster shrugged his shoulders.

An idea suddenly occurred to me. "Thank you," I said, "but you can go back to your shelf."

The rooster did a half bow and promptly returned to its place.

What if it wasn't all me? What if the shop had its own special brand of enchantment?

To test my theory, I needed to leave the building. My keys were still in my pocket, so I walked out of the shop and across the street to the bench by the Confederate Veterans' monument. I sat and looked around to make sure no one was watching. Focusing on a broken branch lying under the hickory tree to my left, I put out my hand and tried to pull the stick toward me. Nothing.

"Hey," I said. "You. The crooked stick with the busted end. Can you come over here, please?"

Nothing.

I tried for fifteen minutes before I went back to the shop. Closing and locking the door, my eye fell on a cane fishing pole in the corner by a rack of t-shirts. I extended my hand, and said, "Come here." In five seconds, I was holding the pole in my hand, watching the red-and-white bobber sway slightly on six inches of loose green cord.

A funny sense of elation tickled in the pit of my stomach. For the first time since I woke up that morning, I felt moderately in control of my world. Summoning my courage, I looked at the pole and said, "Thank you. Can you put yourself in the storeroom, please?"

I felt a slight tugging pressure in my hand. When I released my grip, the pole navigated through the tables and display cases and disappeared into the storeroom.

So that was how Aunt Fiona always knew what was in the shop. She asked!

All those times she disappeared toward the back of the store muttering, she wasn't searching her memory, she was talking to the shop. Now we were getting somewhere!

I moved to the center of the room. "Okay," I said to the space around me. "I think I'm starting to catch on. What if I asked you to quietly show me the eucalyptus oil? Like we had a customer, and I didn't want them to know?"

At first, I thought the shop ignored me, but then off to my left I heard a discreet cough. When I looked a beam of sunlight illuminated a tiny bottle in a glass case. When I opened the door and took out the bottle, the label read, "Oil of Eucalyptus."

I did inherit a magic shop, but not in the way I thought. I still didn't know if Aunt Fiona used the crystals or dried herbs to cast spells or mix potions but whatever she did, the shop was her partner.

When Tori showed at 6:30, I could hardly contain my excitement. I started to babble almost before she made it through the door.

Understand that the conversation would have turned out much different with one of my saner friends. Insanity ranks as one of Tori's better qualities. Other than commanding me to slow down and start at the beginning, she stood right there and listened.

The idea of Aunt Fiona's ghost paying me a visit that morning didn't phase Tori in the least. If anything, she sounded relieved.

"Thank God Fiona got out of that pink polyester pantsuit," Tori said vehemently. "I cannot believe your mom expected her own sister to waltz up to the Pearly Gates in that monstrosity."

That stopped my flow of words cold. "Oh Lord," I said. "Does all this mean there isn't a heaven?"

Tori rolled her eyes. "Oh, no you don't," she said. "I didn't drive all the way over here for you to get all philosophical on me. Did Fiona look upset about being here? I mean she wasn't rattling chains or anything was she?"

"No. When I asked her if she planned to visit again, she said she'd be too busy leading her new afterlife."

"Then leave it at that," Tori said firmly. "I don't think we need to tackle heaven and hell right now. If she said she's not coming back, what's the problem? And why are we standing at the front door?"

"Oh," I said, remembering my manners. "I'm sorry. Come upstairs."

Tori picked up her bag, and we started for the staircase. "As much as I hate to agree with your mom about anything," she said, "this place really is a rat's nest."

"I don't think we should say that anymore," I suggested diplomatically.

"Why not?" Tori asked. "Who exactly are we going to offend?"

"The shop's resident adorable rat, Rodney."

"No!" Tori gasped, her face lighting up. "Where is he?"

"Follow me."

Tori put her stuff down on the bottom step and came with me to the storeroom. I left a light burning on the desk. Rodney probably possessed great night vision, but even a rat likes a night-light.

"Rodney?" I called. "Come meet Tori."

I heard the same rustling sound and in seconds, Rodney's pink nose peeked out between the liniment cans.

"It's okay," I said. "She won't hurt you."

At that, Rodney put his whole head out, and Tori started cooing, her reaction to pretty much any critter on earth, including the skunk she carried home when we were ten. Miraculously, Stinky never sprayed her, but I don't think her mother ever got over the fear that he would.

Stinky lived in the woods right out their back door and would come when Tori called his name. In time, he added Mrs. Stinky and the Stinkettes to the family. The kids went off to skunk college in time, but Stinky and the Missus grew old and died in the backyard where they now lie peacefully under pet tombstones Tori ordered from the *Lillian Vernon* catalog.

Tori took one look at Rodney and said, "Oh my *gawd*, you are the most handsome rat I have ever seen in my whole life!"

Rodney perked up, puffing out his chest and straightening his whiskers. It was all I could do to convince Tori not to bring him upstairs. She might be the Critter Whisperer, but I couldn't see even her skills overcoming the rodent-driven instincts of four big tomcats.

Leaving Rodney safely in his freshly-cleaned bachelor pad, we started upstairs. About halfway up, Tori said, as if the idea just occurred to her, "Why did you ask Aunt Fiona's ghost if she was coming back? Did you *want* her to haunt you?"

"Not haunt, help," I replied as we went into the apartment.

At the sight of Tori, the cats came running. She scooped each one up in turn and then wound up sitting cross-legged on the floor in the middle of the herd. I let them have their reunion. The gang knew "Aunt" Tori from kittenhood. She was responsible for my adoption of Winston and Xavier.

Tori rescued both cats from the alley behind the cafe and brought them to my house.

"Why me?" I asked as I reached for the two bedraggled kittens. "Why do I get to be the crazy cat lady?"

Never mind that "crazy cat lady" had been my personal life calling since mom gave me my first kitten when I was a year old.

"I still have hopes of a social life, Jinksy," Tori told me, busily setting up a new litter box.

Now, watching her, and knowing her history with men, I thought it wouldn't take more than a set of soulful green eyes and a plaintive meow to get her in the tribe with the rest of us. Not to mention the fact that "crazy cat lady" wasn't nearly the turnoff to guys that "crazy skunk lady" would be.

Tori might have her mind on petting my cats, but her attention was still firmly on our conversation. "What did you want Fiona to help you with?" she asked.

To the considerable delight of the cats, I sat down on the floor, too. "Okay," I said. "It's easier to show you."

Aunt Fiona kept a stack of magazines lying on the coffee table. I knew the top one was last week's *People*, so I concentrated on the cover image and beckoned with my hand.

My afternoon practice revealed several insights. If I didn't know the location of an object or if it was in the building, I could ask the store.

So far, the only thing I'd stumped the place on was a request for a pair of men's suspenders in blue. The store produced a set in red and let out a sort of apologetic two-note chime to signal its awareness of the substitution. Had anyone been with me at the time, they would have thought they were hearing the bell over the door.

If, however, I did know the location, could picture the object, or happened to be looking at the thing, I could move it with hand gestures and concentration. Imagine being able to stretch your arm all the way across the room to pick something up. That's what it feels like.

While Tori and the cats watched, I brought the *People* magazine across the room and deposited it in Tori's lap.

Tori looked down at the cover for a minute and then said, "I cannot believe how trashy Miley has gotten. I do not know how Billy Ray puts up with it. That little gal needs a whupping."

"That's it?" I said, stunned. "I just levitate a magazine across the room, and you're worried about Miley Cyrus being trashy?"

"Only because I can't even talk about Blake and Miranda without crying," she said seriously.

"You do know what this means?" I pressed.

"That Johnny and June were country music's last great love story?" she asked with fake, innocent eyes.

"Tori."

"Yeah, Jinksy, I know what it means. You're a witch like Aunt Fiona."

"Well, you're sure taking the news calmly," I said dryly.

"Jinx Hamilton," she said firmly, "I have known you my whole life, and you don't have a wicked bone in your body. I love you exactly the way you are. Now tell me everything."

Chapter Six

"Everything" included my visit with Chase McGregor and his offer to bring us lunch tomorrow and help with any heavy lifting. When Tori asked if Chase was hot, I conceded he raises the temperature in the room.

"Have you dug around looking for Fiona's spell book?" Tori asked, her eyes alight with excitement. "We could seriously make use of some love spells."

Oh, Lord. Something else I hadn't thought about.

Tori frowned when she saw my expression. "What? Since when is love a bad idea? Especially with a hot cat-loving guy living right next door?"

"What if Chase is under a spell already?" I asked uneasily. "What if that's why he was so nice to Aunt Fiona, and they had that whole 'knock on the pipes' code and everything?"

"Girl," Tori said sagely, "you think too much."

"Maybe," I said, rubbing Zeke's ears, "but this is all a lot to take in."

Tori gave me an odd look. "You really didn't know Fiona was a witch?"

I looked up. "Like what, you did?"

"Uh, yeah."

She made it sound like the most obvious information in the world.

"You did not," I groused, realizing the minute the words were out of my mouth how mature they sounded.

"Did, too," Tori answered on cue, grinning.

I rolled my eyes. "Okay. Fine. I'll bite. How did you know Fiona was a witch?"

"Because when we were about ten years old, the moms dropped us off over here for the day because they were going to do something in Sparta," she said. "You remember?"

"Not really."

"You and Fiona went down to George and Irma's. I was playing on the staircase and broke my Barbie mirror."

"My condolences to you and Barbie," I said, "but so what?"

"Aunt Fiona picked the mirror up and handed it back to me," Tori said. "The glass was perfect. I remember looking down at her. She winked at me."

"Aw, come on, Tori," I scoffed. "That's hardly evidence. You must have been wrong about the glass breaking."

"I wasn't," she said stubbornly. "I was already worried about the seven years of bad luck, and then Aunt Fiona made it all okay."

"Did she say anything?"

Tori nodded. "She said, 'Pretty little girls shouldn't have to be worried about bad luck.'"

My throat knotted up and tears filled my eyes. Aunt Fiona might have been an odd duck, but she was also one of the sweetest, most loving human beings I had ever known.

"That sounds like her," I said, clearing my throat and wiping my eyes. "But it still doesn't prove she was a witch."

"Maybe not," Tori said, "but from then on, I watched Aunt Fiona. Did you know she could touch wilted flowers and make them bloom again?"

I was starting to feel like I should get the Miss Oblivious tiara.

"You saw her do that?" I said. "Seriously?"

"Seriously. At your Grandma's funeral. Remember how hot it was in the funeral parlor?"

Did I ever, mainly because before the service started, Daddy observed, rather loudly, that the undertaker made Grandma look so waxy she was going to puddle up and melt in the casket.

That idea scared me so bad I sat through the whole funeral with my eyes glued to the body waiting for Grandma to liquefy.

"Well, the casket spray was started to look droopy when Fiona went up to stand there and say her goodbyes," Tori went on. "I was sitting off to the side. I heard her say, 'We can't send you off with wilted roses, Mama.' She touched the casket spray and those roses all perked right up. Some of the buds even bloomed."

I couldn't believe what I was hearing. "Why didn't you tell me about any of this?"

It was Tori's turn to roll her eyes. "Right, Miss Literal and Logical. Like I'm going to start telling you about your aunt mending mirrors and making flowers bloom. Really, Jinx? You didn't believe in magic of any kind. Not even the everyday stuff that happens all the time, like wishing for a parking spot up front at the mall and getting it."

"That's not magic," I said stubbornly. "It's coincidence."

"See what I mean," she said, sounding vindicated. "What was the point in my telling you what I saw? You have to get hit over the head with a two-by-four, which is kinda what Fiona did this morning showing up like that."

As much as I didn't want to admit that Tori was right, she was right. I sighed. "Okay. You do have a point."

"It's okay, Jinksy," she said, giving me a good-natured tap on the shoulder. "Like I said, I love you just the way you are. But my family are all mountain people. I was raised to believe in haints, and my Granny taught me all the old superstitions."

Clearly, I had a lot to learn. "Like what?"

"Oh, you know, seeing an owl in the daylight means somebody's going to die. Same for hearing a rooster crowing at night or seeing a dog howling while he's looking at the ground."

"Wow," I said, "that's cheerful. Death at every turn."

"The old folks believed that stuff," Tori said seriously. "Most of the superstitions are about avoiding death and not getting hexed. Granny wouldn't cut her hair for fear somebody would use the cut-off parts and put a spell on her. You remember my Great Uncle Nub?"

I nodded. "He used to whittle toy animals for us."

"Right," Tori said. "Well, he witched water wells all over these mountains. He could find water every time with that forked stick of his."

My family came down out of the mountains three or four generations ago. My mother goes to great lengths to distance us from our more folkish roots. She and Aunt Fiona quarreled about that very thing. I said as much to Tori.

"Do you think your mom knew Fiona was a witch?" she asked.

"I have no idea," I said, "but I'm sure as heck not planning on asking her. She'll be dragging me to church and hollering about the devil for a month of Sundays."

Tori nodded sympathetically. We both understood the true mission of all daughters: avoid maternal fits.

"Well, here's what I think," she said. "Aunt Fiona wouldn't

have given you these powers if she didn't think you could handle them. I mean, come on, it's cool, right?"

"I guess," I said uncertainly. "But I'm not going to use magic, so it doesn't make any difference."

"No, no, no, no, no," Tori warned. "You are asking for trouble. It's like going on a diet. As soon as you say you're passing on the fattening food, it rains fried chicken."

That got a laugh out of me. We were both charter members of the Failed Diet of the Month Club. "What do you suggest I do?" I asked. "Come out of the witchy closet and hang up a sign offering to make love potions and read palms?"

"Well, not until you know if you can actually do those things," Tori said seriously. "You're just getting started. Come on. Admit it. Figuring out what you *can* do will be fun. Since Fiona didn't leave instructions, it's like we're going on a magical scavenger hunt."

"That's easy for you to say," I grumbled, but in spite of myself, I felt better about the whole situation.

"Have you talked to any more dead people?" she asked brightly.

Wait! What? *More* dead people?

"No!" I said emphatically. "And I don't want to."

Tori lifted Winston off her lap, stood, and held out her hand. "Well, *I* want you to. Come on."

I took her hand and let her pull me up. "Where are we going?" I asked suspiciously.

"The graveyard."

"Are you crazy? It's almost dark out there," I squawked. "I am not going to the graveyard at night."

"Sure you are," Tori said, completely undeterred by my reaction. "That's when we stand a better chance of seeing spirits."

"What's this '*we*' stuff?" I said. "You can't see ghosts."

"Sure I can."

Oh, for God's sake. "Tori, look," I said, "I know we always do everything together, but how in the world are you going to suddenly start seeing dead people because I can?"

"Duh," she said, "I'll look over your left shoulder."

Well, of course. Why didn't I think of that?

Chapter Seven

I won't lie. We had been to a cemetery in the dark before that night. I will, however, swear on the Good Book that all previous incidents occurred on Halloween. Neither one of us ever egged a tombstone. I plead the Fifth in regard to toilet papering.

The local Briar Hollow cemetery sat on the edge of town on a sloping piece of land that disappeared into deep woods at the north end. The kind of deep woods designed to harbor at least one werewolf and potentially some of those guys from *Deliverance*. In daylight, the graveyard looked peaceful and picturesque; in the dark, I expected a serial killer in a hockey mask to appear any second.

Tori did not help. As the daughters of two dyed-in-the-wool movie buffs, we both possessed an impressive store of screen references. Tori quoted scary movies non-stop until I wished I did know how to hex her.

In my imagination, I expected to walk into a bad remake of *Night of the Living Dead*. What I got was more like *Night at the Museum*.

I don't know what the funeral parlor mixes with formaldehyde, but the people we found were seriously high on death.

The instant I unlatched the rusty iron gate and stepped inside the boundaries of the burying ground, my paranormal rabbit ears pulled in a signal. One minute I saw a moonlit cemetery and the next, a mostly transparent coonhound loped through the grave markers.

As I watched, this so-called "hellhound" vaulted over a praying angel and jumped to pluck a spectral tennis ball out of the air. The dog then trotted obediently back to a Confederate colonel in full uniform while a flapper, two grannies in long gingham dresses, and a woman with a massive beehive and cat's eyeglasses applauded. The dog wagged his tail so vigorously, it acted like a helicopter rotor and lifted him a good foot off the ground.

"Do you see anything?" Tori whispered.

"Uh, yeah," I stammered. "Several anythings."

"Oh my God," she said from behind me and to the left. "Quit hogging the good seats. Scrunch down so I can see, too."

On the drive over she explained to me that, according to her grandmother, if one person saw a ghost that was invisible to a second person, the bystander could peer over the first person's left shoulder and all would be revealed.

Seriously, who comes up with this stuff?

But, being a good sport, and judging from the gasp Tori let out as soon as I "scrunched," her granny must have been right.

"Holy crap," Tori said as we watched a high school football player jog past. "Do you suppose it's like this every night?"

A discreet cough made me turn my head to the right. The Colonel swept off his Panama hat and bowed low. "Good evening, ladies," he said in a deep voice. "Welcome to the evening's festivities."

"Oh. My. God." Tori said, still straining to see over my shoulder. "I can hear them, too."

"Colonel Beauregard T. Longworth at your service, ma'am," the spirit said. "Loitering behind your friend will no longer be necessary. We're all quite happy to allow you to see us."

Tori moved around me and took a cautious step toward the beaming Colonel. "Can I touch you?" she asked.

"You may try," he said, "but I fear you will not be successful."

He called it. Tori's hand passed right through the gold braid on his sleeve. She yelped and jerked back. "Ouch! Colonel Longworth," she exclaimed, "you're ice cold!"

The Colonel chuckled, "Well, my dear, I haven't had a functional circulatory system since 1864. Please, call me Beau." The specter turned to me. "You must be Jinx," he said. "Fiona told us to expect you."

Of course she did.

"You knew . . . er . . . know my aunt?" I asked.

The football player galloped to a stop beside the Colonel and took off his helmet. "We all know Fiona," the boy said enthusiastically. "She's the bee's knees. Every Friday night during the season she'd come out here with a portable radio so I could listen to the high school football game."

"Why don't you just go to the game yourself?" Tori asked. "It's not like you have a curfew or anything."

The boy's expression settled into a perfect picture of teenage annoyance. "Yeah, I kinda do," he said. "None of us can go past the fence."

"Why not?" Tori asked.

"I don't know," the boy said, "but I can prove it to you."

He put his helmet back on, crouched, and charged the cemetery fence. At the last minute he launched himself to hurdle the low barrier. Instead, he smacked into an invisible wall. The impact threw him back where he landed at our feet in a glowing heap. Wrenching his helmet off the kid looked up at Tori and said, "See? I told you."

A small group of spirits formed around us. Each one said something nice about Aunt Fiona. One of the women dressed in gingham told me, "Fiona didn't forget us just because we're dead. She made us feel like we're still part of the community."

An unspoken question hung in the air. What was I going to do for them?

Aunt Fiona didn't burden me with an unwanted gift. She entrusted me with a tremendous responsibility. I smiled at the ghosts and said sincerely, "I'm looking forward to getting to know all of you."

A collective sigh of relief rose from the crowd, stirring the leaves on the tree over our heads. Addressing Colonel Longworth, I said, "Sir, may I have a word with you in private?"

"Why, of course," he replied gallantly. "Forgive me for not offering you my arm, but I am at something of a disadvantage."

"Not at all," I said, falling in beside him as we moved toward a quiet corner. When we were out of earshot of the others, I said, "I hope you won't think I'm being rude, but I'm new to all of this. Why are you all still here with the living?"

Beau looked at me sadly. "You mean why have we not ascended to some celestial realm or descended to a lower place to answer for our sins?"

"Something like that, yeah."

"None of us truly know, Miss Jinx," he admitted. "Some are condemned to walk the earth because we cannot let go of our attachment to the living. Young Jeff there, the lad in the football uniform, fears that if he goes on to whatever is next, he will no longer be able to enjoy his favorite sport. The lady in the blue gingham dress and bonnet has waited for her husband lo these seventy-five years, but he has never come for her."

I hesitated and then said, "And you, sir?"

Drawing himself up to his full height, Beau said, "I cannot leave my post until the Southern states rise from their ignominious defeat at the hands of those blaggard Yankees. The Confederacy must be vindicated and restored as the rightful government of this region."

Oh, yeah. Beau was going to be here a *long* time.

"So basically, you all have some kind of unfinished business?" I ventured diplomatically.

"That is what your aunt believed," he said, "and over the years, she was successful in helping one or two of our number to go elsewhere, but I cannot tell you the details of their destination. She referred to those of us still in residence as the 'hard cases.' In the end, Fiona chose to simply make our existence in this place more interesting. It is quite tedious when the living walk among us and do not even speak, or worse when they do not come at all. Your aunt was quite the breath of fresh air with her acceptance of our non-corporeal state."

That's Aunt Fiona for you. A regular ectoplasmic, tree-hugging liberal.

Before I could ask Beau more questions, Tori hurried over. "Jinx," she said urgently, "you have to meet someone."

Leave it to Tori to work the undead room.

I followed her to a lonely grave in the far corner. She pointed at the granite stone. The etched words read, "Jane Doe, Died in Briar Hollow, 1995. Known Only to God."

Tori's expression looked suspiciously familiar. Intuitively I knew she was about to introduce me to a different kind of stray. She stepped aside to reveal a gossamer-thin entity with enormous eyes. "Jinksy, meet Jane."

Dear God. First homeless skunks and now forlorn ghosts.

"Hi, Jane," I said. "It's nice to meet you."

"Jane isn't my name," the ghost whispered.

Jane couldn't have been more than 18 when she died.

Although I saw her in shades of gray and white, I thought the girl's shoulder-length hair was brown.

"What would you like us to call you?" I asked.

The girl's voice broke. "I don't know my name." The words came out in a low moan. "I don't know anything about myself except someone killed me. Then I woke up here, and I can never leave."

From beside me, Colonel Longworth's sonorous voice said gently, "Fiona called Jane the hardest of her hard cases."

"She doesn't remember how she died?" I asked.

"Worse," the Colonel said, "she cannot name the shiftless brigand who murdered her."

Chapter Eight

Yep. That's right. The Universe thought Jinx and her terrible, horrible, no-good, very bad day she was having needed a little sprinkle of twenty-year-old murder for flavor.

"Miss Fiona theorized that Jane cannot move beyond this earth until her killer faces justice and her name is restored," Colonel Longworth explained.

"Did Aunt Fiona try to solve the murder?" I asked. The Colonel motioned for us to move away so our conversation wouldn't upset the fragile spirit.

"Yes," he said, "but never with success."

"What do you know about how she died?"

"Only that she was felled by a single blow to the head on a local trail in the year nineteen hundred and ninety-five," he said.

I looked around at the ghosts wandering the cemetery. "Why do all of the rest of you seem so . . . well-adjusted?"

"We know who we are," Beau answered, "or rather we know who we were. We can speak with one another of our families and of the lives we lived. We learn as each spirit joins our number. Jane is a blank slate. She remembers nothing of her life."

So, there is a hell—and we were looking at it. Damn.

Tori walked up as the Colonel finished speaking. I saw what she said next coming a mile off.

"Jinx, we have to fix this. We can't leave her here like this."

Glancing at my watch, I said, "Tori, I've had this whole 'powers' thing exactly eighteen hours. How do you think I . . . we . . . are going to fix this exactly?"

"I don't know," she said stubbornly, "but we have to do something."

Beau was beaming at Tori again. I swear I think he was getting sweet on her. "I like your spirit, young lady," he declared. "You are a true daughter of the South."

Since it was getting on toward one in the morning, I suggested that me and Miss Scarlett best get back to the plantation. Beau walked us to the gate.

"If I come here during the day, can I see you all?" I asked him.

"Not all of us," he said. "It would seem we grow more experienced the longer we are on this side. I can appear during daylight hours."

"Where are you when you're not visible?" Tori asked.

The question seemed to briefly confuse the old soldier. "I am always in the same place," he finally said.

Well, okay then. That cleared that right up. Not.

Regaining his composure, Beau said, "Call out to me in the vicinity of my resting place, and I will hear you." He pointed to a tall, white marble obelisk. "That is my marker."

Not exactly like a guy giving you his number on a cocktail napkin, but close enough.

"Thank you, Colonel Longworth," I said.

"Beau," he corrected me again. He reached for my hand, which I held up in approximately the right location. Gallant gentleman that he was, Longworth pretended to kiss my hand. I didn't feel his lips, but a cool breeze passed over my skin.

The instant Tori and I stepped through the gate, the cemetery became dark and deserted again.

"That," Tori declared, "was a *total* trip."

It was a short drive back to the shop. Four indignant cats greeted us unamused over being left alone until the wee morning hours. We changed into our pajamas and settled on opposite ends of the sofa with super-sized glasses of red wine and a big bowl of popcorn between us.

"So now what?" I said.

"You're asking me?" Tori replied. "Can't you make a 911 call to Fiona?"

"I've tried," I grimaced. "I think she's sending me straight to voicemail. Okay. So." I scanned my brain. "What would Buffy do?"

"Ask Giles," Tori said. "Duh."

In the absence of a smart British guy, we went the next best route. We Googled.

Colonel Longworth related the basic details accurately. Jane's body was found lying beside a hiking trail about five miles outside the city limits. The coroner estimated she was 18 years old, but neither the body nor the tattered backpack discovered nearby offered up any clues about her identity.

A single blow to the head killed her. The body was in an advanced state of decomposition and. . . well . . . *animals* . . . enough said. A sketch artist rendered a likeness based on cranial measurements. The image on the screen easily matched the features of the young ghost.

National news outlets ran the picture, but no one recognized Jane, and she didn't fit the description of any missing person. After several months, the people of Briar Hollow asked for permission to bury the body in the local cemetery.

The town took up a collection to pay for the funeral, and

from what we could tell, the whole community attended. That choked me up. Only kind strangers mourned the unfortunate girl.

"Aunt Fiona must have gone to the service," I said. "She was probably already talking to Jane's ghost during the investigation."

"Do you remember hearing anything about this when it happened?" Tori asked, reaching for a handful of popcorn.

"No. But you know our moms. They never wanted us to know about anything bad going on in the world. We were nine when Jane was found. They probably thought hearing about a local murder would freak us out."

Tori munched thoughtfully, washing the popcorn down with more wine. "This could explain why they wouldn't let us hike that part of the Appalachian Trail."

"We would have starved to death in an abandoned school bus like that guy in the movie," I snorted. "Neither one of us was outdoorsy enough to hike anywhere."

"We were kids," Tori laughed. "We had big ideas." Then she grew quiet. "Just like Jane. She can't even remember what her dreams were, Jinksy. That's not right. What about her people? They don't even know where she's buried."

Tori was preaching to the choir. We would help Jane, even if I didn't know how. The effects of a long day, too much excitement, three glasses of wine, and a ton of popcorn caught up with me. I let out a yawn so strong, I swear the easy chair on the other side of the room scooted forward.

"Yeah, me too," Tori said, responding with a contagious yawn of her own.

I managed to stumble to bed. Tori sacked out on the sofa with the cats under one of Aunt Fiona's crocheted afghans.

The cats let us sleep. At nine o'clock the aroma of brewing coffee brought Tori's head off the pillow. "Morning," she mumbled. "Did you remember to get me my half-and-half?"

"Good morning to you, too," I answered from the kitchen. "Your congealed dairy sludge is waiting for you."

I heard her get up and pad to the bathroom. When she appeared in the kitchen and stumbled over to one of the chairs at the table, I couldn't keep from laughing at her bedhead. The woman looked like she could tune in Radio Free Mars without the benefit of a tinfoil cap.

With a cup of coffee in each hand, I joined her. Tori added sugar and half-and-half to her morning elixir. Half a cup later, she emerged from her bleary post-sleep fugue state a different woman.

"Well," I said, "there you are."

She grinned. "Just needed a little caffeinated jumpstart. So, what's the plan?"

"The same as yesterday," I said. "We get downstairs and go to work."

"But what about Jane?" Tori protested. "We have to figure out who killed her."

Right. Solve a 20-year-old murder by noon. Piece of cake.

"In case you've forgotten, a handsome man offered to bring us lunch today."

Tori's eyes brightened. "Oh! That's right!"

"This would be the same handsome man who was Aunt Fiona's friend," I pointed out. "If she had an interest in Jane's unsolved murder, Chase would know about it."

"Good thinking," Tori admitted, "but how are you going to work Jane into the conversation? Casually mention we went for a walk in the cemetery at midnight and ran into her?"

"I'm one ahead of you on that one, too," I said. "Get dressed and come downstairs with me."

We took turns in the tiny bathroom and made ourselves more presentable than we normally would on a Saturday that involved taking inventory, but hey, see previous reference regarding 'handsome man.'

An hour later, we stood in the middle of the shop. I hadn't bothered to flip on the light. Dust-filled shafts of sunshine from the big front windows illuminated the space. I cleared my throat. "Good morning . . . shop," I said.

Tori snickered and I gave her "the look." She quieted down and arranged her features in a more serious expression.

I started again. "I was wondering if you could help me with something. Do you have anything about the girl who was killed outside of town on the hiking trail in 1995?"

The grinding of gears answered me, followed by a "ding." A drawer in one of the display cases slid open. Tori and I peered inside and saw a manila folder. When I extracted it and opened the file, I found newspaper clippings covering Jane's case.

"There you go," I said. "One conversation starter with Chase McGregor."

"This is freaking cool!" Tori said. She looked around. "Shop, you're awesome!" Then she thought for a minute and said, "Do you have a name?"

My laughter died in my throat when the blackboard by the front door spun around on its nail a few times before coming to a stop. "Call me Myrtle," was written in perfect block letters in the center of the board.

Myrtle the Magical Shop?

"Now you're messing with us," I said in an accusatory voice.

I kid you not, the store giggled.

Chapter Nine

"Why can I see and hear all this stuff?" Tori asked, dragging a box of Christmas elf ornaments off a shelf and starting to count them.

"I guess the metaphysical management figures you're with me," I said, making an entry on our running list for "brass spittoons - four."

Tori finished her count and said, "Thirteen elves and one misplaced green garden gnome."

Adding them to the list, I asked, "Are you okay with all this?"

"Are you kidding me?" Tori said, opening the stepladder. "This is freaking fantastically awesome, Jinksy! Ghosts and witch powers and Myrtle. This is *way* better than winning the lottery and buying mom a new double-wide."

That cracked me up. We had a long-running joke about the bizarrely predictable acquisitions of lottery winners. A new double-wide for mom occupied the top three, along with dually trucks, and trashy women (or worthless handsome men, as the case might be).

After Myrtle produced the folder of newspaper clippings,

we looked through the material without finding any new information. Knowing the store would help calmed my inventory panic, and I was able to both tidy up and showcase our hard work for Chase.

Tori turned on the full force of her organizational skills. The antique display case inside the front door slowly emerged as a center for essential oils and herbal products. Tori stopped from time to time for a quick Google search. At her direction I called a local soap maker to discuss carrying her all natural, vegan creations.

About ten minutes after noon, Chase tapped on the front door. As I went to let him in, Tori, talking like a bad ventriloquist, said, "Exactly why have I never met this man before today?"

Responding in kind through my smile, I said, "He's only been running the leather shop three or four years. It's been at least that long since you've come over here with me to visit."

"You didn't tell me I was missing a hunk of *that* quality," she mumbled. "You only talked about his cat."

There was a good reason for that. I could express an interest in a cat without anyone making a big deal about it. Let me mention a good-looking man and suddenly everyone around me wanted to know if I was "serious." It takes more than a handsome face for me to get interested in a guy. So far, I liked what I knew about Chase, but more investigation was in order.

For the record, I'm not exactly a mud fence in the looks department. Mom tells me it won't last, but so far, I can eat whatever I want without gaining serious weight. I take after her side of the family—round features but with a good jawline and a nice nose. The sun puts red highlights in my dark hair. I've always thought I'm okay but not anything to write home about.

Guys look at Tori before they notice me. Her blue eyes dance with good humor. That day she wore her strawberry blonde hair in a cute, spikey pixie cut tinged in magenta on the ends. I'm about five feet eight, and she's struggling to make five feet, compensating with pure personality and enthusiasm for life.

Tori comes up with the bright ideas. She wants to zip line; I ask for the date of the last safety check on the harnesses. I'll get on the dang zip line, but I need to see the paperwork in triplicate first.

It surprised me when Chase smiled warmly at Tori and then turned the full force of his gaze back to me. "How are you getting settled in?" he asked.

When a warm flash washed over my body, I mentally blamed the afternoon sun for superheating the shop. "Oh," I said, "you know how it goes. The cats are happy, therefore, I am happy."

Chase answered in the universal tone of cat loving commiseration, "Do I ever. I built a set of stairs so Festus can get on the bed without help. He wouldn't use them until I switched out the rubber tread for carpet. He gave me that whole 'good help is so hard to find' look."

He built his lame cat a set of stairs to get on the bed? Oh. My. God. I could possibly be staring at the perfect man.

From beside me, Tori, fully tuned in to the undercurrent of developing subtext between Chase and me, said, "How'd Festus come up lame?"

"He was born with a deformed hip," Chase said. "Nobody would adopt him at the shelter. They were going to put him down. I couldn't let that happen. Trust me, when he gets the zoomies at three o'clock in the morning, he does fine on three legs."

I couldn't believe what I was hearing. "Festus gets the zoomies?" I asked incredulously. "Why does he always limp so bad and meow to be picked up when I see him?"

Chase flashed me a grin. "He's a cat," he said. "A *man* cat. He knows how to work the angles."

We all laughed, and Tori telegraphed me a silent BFF communique, "*He's a keeper. Go for it.*"

God love my girl, she doesn't have a jealous bone in her body. It would never enter her mind to shift into competition mode because a guy showed interest in me.

"I don't mean to sound rude or anything," she said to Chase, "but I heard you were going to come bearing pizzas."

"I come bearing the menu from the pizzeria," Chase replied, taking a folded piece of paper out of the pocket of his jeans. "I didn't want to run the risk of showing up with anything you all wouldn't like."

Fat chance. I'd eat tofu if Chase McGregor handed it to me.

We all conferred over the menu, and Chase wrote down what we wanted. When Tori asked why he didn't phone the order in, Chase explained that the owner ran a one-man show and didn't have time to answer calls.

We watched Chase cross the courthouse square with long, loping strides, like a man on a mission. Tori let out a low whistle. "That boy is *fine*," she said appreciatively. "I'm with Fiona. He can knock on my pipes anytime."

"He is cute, isn't he?" I ventured shyly.

"Cute does not do justice to that," Tori said, grinning. "He likes you."

"You think?" I asked doubtfully.

"I think."

"We'll see," I said. The reticence was for show. Inside I was turning cartwheels.

Chase returned with three medium pizzas and a small sack of double fudge brownies. "I don't know how it happened," he explained innocently. "They jumped into my hand."

"Thank God you caught them before they hurt someone,"

I said solemnly. "That's the trouble with chocolate. It's so aggressive."

We went into the storeroom to make use of the table and chairs. To my surprise, Chase called out, "Hey Rodney," as he put the boxes down.

The resident rat immediately stuck his head out and wiggled his whiskers in greeting.

"You know about Rodney?" I asked, opening one of the pizza boxes and almost swooning at the heavenly aroma that wafted.

"Sure I do," Chase said, breaking off a piece of crust and offering it to the rat. "We're old buddies."

My eyes must have been playing tricks on me. I could have sworn Rodney high fived the tip of Chase's index finger before accepting the crust and taking it to his room.

"So, what's Rodney's story?" Tori asked, biting into a slice. "Did Fiona get him at a pet store or something?"

Wiping his chin with a napkin, Chase said, "No. It was the darnedest thing. Somebody left Rodney on the front step in his cage one morning. Festus found him when I opened up, and Fiona came out to see what was going on. She insisted on keeping Rodney for his own safety."

"Did Festus try to turn him into a snack?" I asked.

"Actually, no," Chase said. "If anything, it looked like the two of them were having a conversation through the bars of the cage, but I wasn't willing to risk it." Then, as if the idea had just occurred to him, he added, "Uh, how many cats do you have?"

"Four," I said, "and trust me, this will be a segregated household."

Chase looked relieved. "Good," he said. "Rodney will grow on you fast. I swear he's going to talk one of these days."

"Why did Fiona put the cage behind those liniment cans?" Tori asked.

"Huh," Chase said. "I don't know. Fiona always had her own way of doing things."

That was an opening if I ever heard one.

"She did, didn't she?" I said, preparing to steer the conversation in a new direction. "I've been finding all kinds of things I didn't know she was interested in, including true crime."

"True crime?" Chase asked, frowning. "What do you mean?"

Earlier I strategically placed the manila folder on the worktable. I leaned over and snagged it and put it in front of Chase.

"We found this file of newspaper articles this morning," I said. "Fiona must have been interested in this unsolved murder."

Chase opened the folder and shook his head. "Ah, Jane Doe," he said. "Everyone in town knows about her. I wasn't here when it happened, but Fiona told me about the investigation. Every year on the anniversary people go out and put flowers on the grave. In fact, that's coming up in a couple of weeks."

"Why was Fiona so interested?" I asked.

"You don't know?" Chase said. "The girl came in the store about a week before her body was discovered."

"No way," Tori said. "What happened?"

"Not much, according to Fiona," Chase said, extracting another slice of pizza from his box. "The girl was dressed for hiking. She stopped at George and Irma's to get food for the trail. When she walked by here, she saw a quartz necklace in the window and came in to ask the price. Fiona asked her how much she had to spare, and the girl said five dollars. Fiona told her she was in luck because that was how much the necklace cost. The girl wore it out of the store."

That was Fiona. Softest heart in the world.

"Aunt Fiona didn't get her name?" I asked.

"No," Chase said. "That haunted Fiona. There were a lot

of tourists in here that day, and Fiona was too busy to visit with the girl. I think Fiona blamed herself. She always said if she'd just gotten the poor kid's first name, maybe the police could have gotten better leads. She was upset about the necklace."

"What about the necklace?" Tori asked.

"It wasn't on the body or in the backpack," Chase said. "Fiona worried someone on the trail thought it was valuable and killed the girl to steal it. The stone was plain quartz. Nothing special. The body was found by a creek up near Weber's Gap. For some reason, Fiona was convinced the necklace wound up in the water. She went up there several times trying to find it."

"Why would she do that if it wasn't valuable?"

"Beats me," Chase said. "Fiona said if she could find the necklace, she'd know what happened. It didn't make any sense to me, but again, it was Fiona. She always came at things her own way." He wiped his fingers and reached for the brown sack, "Anybody else think it's brownie time?"

Chapter Ten

Chase helped us all afternoon. I have to confess those fudge brownies disappeared. By the time he excused himself for the evening and went home, the store showed signs of order. Chase told me about several regional artisans who made everything, from musical instruments to furniture.

How I managed to ignore such craftsmen my whole life I do not know, but thanks to him, my potential inventory list grew exponentially. The day left me more enthused about being a shopkeeper and less worried about being a witch.

Alone again, Tori and I discussed the information Chase shared about Aunt Fiona and her real interest in Jane's case.

"So, what do you think the deal was about the necklace?" Tori asked. "Is there some mojo associated with quartz?"

"You're asking me?" I said. "I barely have my junior mojo membership card. Other than the story I told you about Aunt Fiona giving that widow the rose quartz necklace, I know nothing about the stuff."

We were still downstairs, so Tori cleared her throat and

said, "Uh, Myrtle? Would it be okay if I asked you a question?"

The store answered with a happy three-note trill we took as a yes.

"Okay, thanks," Tori said. "Is there more quartz in the store?"

That same spotlight, out of nowhere, instantly highlighted a shelf in the jewelry counter near the front window. We both leaned down to look and saw a pair of earrings, a necklace, and a ring, all set with clear stones. Unfortunately, none of them obligingly stepped up to explain why we should think of them as anything but . . . rocks.

Since we'd worked up an appetite again, we thanked Myrtle and went upstairs to consult the Internet while chowing down on mac n' cheese. Until that night, my previous experience with paranormal research amounted to watching *Charmed* and owning the DVD of *Practical Magic*. The number of websites dedicated to the topic shocked me. Some I found disturbing.

Before we started reading about beliefs associated with crystals, I hadn't thought about expanding my stock in that direction, but that changed fast. Crystals are seriously popular. Enthusiasts regard pure quartz as the universal crystal. Quartz can be found virtually everywhere and works as a multipurpose stone for positive protection.

We also found plenty of references to rose quartz as well. The stone heals broken hearts. That night, my thoughts ran along the lines of, "*Hey, if people want to buy rocks, I'm more than happy to sell them rocks.*"

I no longer mock crystals, but we'll get to that.

When found in proximity to running water, quartz acts like a writable DVD. Jane's necklace could have recorded her murder.

"You think that's it?" Tori asked. "Fiona thought the necklace could tell her what happened to Jane?"

"Maybe," I said. "That's assuming Fiona knew how to hit the play button on the rock—which I would ask her if she'd freaking answer my calls."

That last annoyed comment makes it sound like I picked up my cell phone and speed dialed my dead aunt. Mainly I looked at the ceiling and begged her to float in.

Upstairs, I attempted to get Fiona to join the party. The effort did nothing but cause the cats to stare at me like I'd lost what little intelligence they ever thought I possessed. (Which, for you non-cat people, counts as precious little on a good day.)

"Aw, come on, lay off Aunt Fiona," Tori said, uncorking a fresh bottle of red wine. "She obviously trusts you to figure this all out, including what happened to Jane. Why don't we go up to the hiking trail in the morning and see if we can find anything?"

Like I didn't see that one coming.

"Tori, Jane died twenty years ago," I said, pointing out what should have been obvious. "The cops have been all over that trail hundreds of times. Anything they were going to find, they found years ago. What do you think we're going to see that they didn't?"

"I don't know," Tori said, handing me a full wine glass. "But don't we owe it to Jane to see where she was found? It seems respectful given her current situation. Besides, you don't know everything you can do yet. Maybe you *will* see something Fiona didn't. Not all witches are alike, right?"

Truthfully, I had no idea if that was true or not, but the notion made sense.

We finished the evening playing a cutthroat game of Settlers of Catan and turned in around midnight. The next morning, the smell of frying bacon awakened me. I walked into the kitchen to discover Tori fixing her to-die-for western omelets.

"Hey," I said, "where'd all this come from?"

"Irma and George are open on Sunday mornings," she said. "I woke up early and slipped down to the corner. Coffee?"

"Lord, yes," I said, taking the cup she held out. "Thanks. You're bribing me to go up to the trail, aren't you?"

Uh, yeah. I saw through the BFF breakfast when I smelled the bacon.

Tori laughed. "Okay. Busted. Did it work?"

I sighed. "Yeah, I guess we're taking a field trip."

Since Tori didn't have to leave until late afternoon, we took our time. Props to my girl. Her skills with eggs and shredded cheese are awesome. By the time we dressed and I cleaned up the kitchen, we set out for Weber's Gap around eleven o'clock.

As hiking trails go, this one was definitely a bunny slope. Tori and I strolled leisurely up the gentle grade enjoying the bright sunshine and the crisp, clean air. We weren't exactly sure where Jane's body was found. Then we rounded a bend and came on a simple, rough-hewn stone with the inscription, "Here an unknown soul was lost."

"Wow," Tori said, "maybe nobody knows Jane's real name, but she's sure hasn't been forgotten."

I leaned down to examine the marker, tripped on an exposed root, and fell toward the stone. The second my hand made contact with the marker the world became a confused, swirling mass of color.

When my vision cleared, I stood in a vast, empty space with a black, shiny object coming straight at me. Pain shot through my left temple, and then I heard Tori's voice.

Blinking and reaching for my head, I realized I was sitting on the ground with Tori crouched beside me.

"Jinksy," she asked in a worried voice, "are you okay? What the heck happened?"

"Yeah," I said slowly, still getting my bearings. "I'm okay."

"Did you have a dizzy spell or something?" Tori asked. "God, I hope that ham I put in the omelets wasn't bad. I wasn't trying to poison us."

"You didn't poison us," I assured her. "I think I had a vision of where Jane was killed, and it wasn't here."

"Get *out*!" Tori said excitedly. "A vision? What did you see? Where was she killed? Tell me everything!"

"I'm not sure where it was. There was a lot of empty space around me and this . . . thing . . . coming at my head," I answered, rubbing my forehead. "I actually felt it hit me, and then everything went black. It looked familiar. I should know what it was, but I can't quite put my finger on it."

From behind us, a voice said, "It was a tripod, wasn't it?"

Tori and I both swiveled around.

"Who said that?" Tori asked, swinging her head from side to side.

"She did," I answered.

"She who?" Tori asked, perplexed.

"Left shoulder," I directed.

Tori shifted and looked again. "Aw crud," she said. "Jane wasn't the only one."

The ghost of a young girl stood at the edge of the forest. "Who is Jane?" she asked, frowning.

"Someone we know who is like you," I said. "What's your name, honey?"

The girl looked like she was about to cry. "I don't know," she said forlornly. "Every time I try to ask someone, they either don't seem to hear me, or they run away like I scared them." She faltered for a second and then blurted out, "Am I dead?"

Trust me. There are moments when this talking-to-dead-people thing is not all it's cracked up to be. Dead or not, they have feelings.

"Yes," I said gently. "You are."

The girl began to cry softly, “Do you think someone has told my mother?”

“I honestly don’t know,” I said. “Do you have any idea how long you’ve been here?”

The girl shook her head.

“What’s the last thing you remember?” I asked.

She made a face, “That awful new Coca-Cola. I drank a can and thought I would throw up.”

Tori took out her phone and started typing. After a couple of minutes, she looked up and said, “1985.”

Ten years before Jane was killed. Not good. Not good at all.

Chapter Eleven

"We have to report this," Tori said in a low voice as we both watched the nameless girl wander around the clearing.

"And say what?" I asked. "Yes, Officer? I'd like to report a 30-year-old haunting up by Weber's Gap."

Tori made a face. "Very funny," she said. "There could be more dead girls up here. We may be standing in a serial killer's dumping ground."

She said that like discovering such a gruesome truth would be a good thing. Personally, I wanted to get the heck out of there before any more ghosts showed up. Of course, I was far too responsible to do that, but I thought about it—seriously.

"Do you have a bright idea about how to go about this?" I asked.

"It's really not going to be that hard, "Tori said confidently. "You hear about this kind of thing all the time. People go for a walk in the woods and stumble on a body, or a skeleton."

"Note to self," I muttered, "stay out of the woods. That's all well and good, Tori, but we didn't find her body so what exactly do we report?"

"That's the part of the plan she has to help us with," Tori said, nodding toward the girl.

"Help us how?"

"We have to ask her."

I had a sneaking suspicion Tori was being intentionally obtuse because she knew I wasn't going to like the next part.

"Ask her what?" I said suspiciously.

"To show us what's . . . left . . . of herself."

Oh. *Ouch.* Miss Manners had zero etiquette rules to cover that conversation.

"How do you suggest we broach the subject of her mortal remains?" I hissed. "Not five minutes ago she asked us for confirmation that she's actually dead."

"Exactly," Tori said. "Confirmation. She knew, she just didn't *want* to know."

Which, when you think about it, was a perfectly reasonable reaction.

When I didn't say anything, Tori continued. "We ask her, or rather, *you* ask her," she said, hastily correcting herself. "You're the official witch after all."

And there it was, under the wheels of the bus I went.

"I'll do it," I shot back. "But you totally owe me."

As we approached her, the young girl turned toward us. "I want to see my mom," she said. "I need to know she's okay about all this."

A request that in no way made my job easier. But it did give me an opening to wade in as delicately as I could manage.

"We can't take you to your mom until we figure out who you are," I said. "We have to report your death to the police. To do that we need what's . . . I mean where your . . . if there's anything . . ."

My strong start petered off into incoherence. The words took a wrong turn at the corner of Awkward and Embarrassing and jittered to a stop somewhere between Stutter and Tourette's.

The girl cocked her head to one side as if trying to decipher a foreign language. Then her eyes brightened. "Oh," she said. "You want to see my bones."

That sounded way more ghoulish when someone finally said it out loud.

"We don't *want* to see your bones," I said emphatically, "but we have to so we can show the police where you are, and they can start an investigation."

"Okay," the girl said as if the request was the most normal thing in the world. "Follow me."

We watched as she glided off toward the merrily tinkling trout stream that ran parallel to the trail. In daylight the girl's spirit was so transparent, she almost looked like a wisp of fog floating over the landscape.

Tori and I both stared at the prominent "Stay on the Path" sign, shrugged, and set off after our ghostly tour guide.

We hopped over without missing a step. The bank sloped gently upward on the far side, ending at the tree line. The instant we moved into the cover of the forest, the temperature dropped a few degrees. A different kind of stillness settled around us.

For me, at least, there is no quiet so utterly peaceful as the deep woods. It's a space that manages to be both alive with activity and utterly deserted at the same time. The soft soil naturally muted our footsteps, but Tori and I had both been taught by our mothers to walk quietly in nature. My mom watches birds, and Gemma loves wildlife photography. Both hobbies require a degree of stealth.

As we followed the nameless girl who walked—or really glided—farther into the trees, the birds continued to sing. Overhead squirrels played in the branches, and I even caught sight of a deer far off to one side, peering at us warily.

Can you say surreal?

After about five minutes, the girl stopped beside a fallen hickory so far gone into decay, thick ferns covered what remained of the trunk. In another year or two the felled tree would be just another lump of soft mulch on the forest floor. Mother Nature uses every death as potential nourishment for new life.

"I'm in there," the girl said simply, pointing to the exposed roots of the moldering tree.

We walked around to the back of the hickory. You couldn't tell from the front, but the trunk was hollowed out down to the mass of roots. I leaned over and looked inside, but I couldn't see anything.

Tori took out her phone and switched the flashlight app on. When she shined the beam into the interior, a yellowed skull looked back at us.

"How did she get in there?" I said in a low voice.

"I was under the tree," the girl said helpfully. "Then it fell down. So now I'm inside."

"Loose translation," Tori said, "the killer buried her at the base of the tree, which continued to grow. When the tree fell over, the skeleton was tangled up in the roots."

"Right," I agreed, "that makes sense, but how are we going to sell the cops on the idea that we stumbled on a skeleton *inside* a hollowed-out tree trunk?"

"We use iPhone-ography," Tori said triumphantly.

"Excuse me?"

"I enter contests online with photos I take on my iPhone," she said. "That's exactly the kind of thing I'd take a picture for the 'Signs of Decay' contest this month."

She pointed at an uneven row of mushrooms growing along the top of the hickory's trunk.

"Watch this," Tori said, maneuvering to get an angle with

her phone's camera. Even though it was broad daylight, she forced the flash to fire.

"Why did you do that?" I asked.

"If anybody asks me," Tori said, "I'm going to say I was using a fill flash to compensate for sunlight behind the mushrooms that would make my picture dark. But the real reason I used the flash was so we could see this."

She held out her phone. When I looked at the screen, she pinched the image to enlarge it. The skull practically glowed in the dark.

"Good one," I said admiringly. "Gemma would be proud of you. So, what's the story?"

Did I mention Tori handles the alibis? She's the fast thinker.

"We wandered off the path, totally breaking the rules because I'm dying to win the photo contest, which I am, by the way," she explained. "I took some pictures of the mushrooms and when we got back to the trail, I sat down to look at them, and I saw the skull."

This would be why we've always been able to get away with pretty much anything. Tori keeps her stories simple and close enough to the truth that we're not so much lying as bending the facts.

"That should work," I said. "But we have to wait a while before we go to the sheriff. Those picture files will have a date and time stamp."

Now it was her turn to be proud of me. "Listen to you, all in secret agent mode!" she said. "Double-O Jinksy."

From the other side of the hickory, the girl said plaintively, "Excuse me for interrupting, but what about me? What am I going to do now?"

How could I tell her that she was never actually going to *do* anything again?

Tori and I both looked at the girl and then at one another. I saw it coming in Tori's eyes before she even said a word. Both of my hands went up to fend off the bad idea barreling straight at me.

"No," I said firmly. "She is *not* coming home with us."

The girl spoke again before Tori could start wheedling.

"Please don't leave me here," the ghost said, her voice cracking. "I've been alone for so long. You're the first people I've talked to who have answered me since I woke up in this place."

God. It's bad enough when a dog or a cat gives you the please-don't-leave-me eyes. How do you turn down the spirit of a murdered teenager turned middle-aged haunt? There's no walking away from that kind of sadness and living with yourself afterward.

The sigh I let out was equal parts resignation and genuine sympathy. "Okay," I said, "you can come with us . . ."

Looking back on that moment now, I realize I should have said, "try to come with us" because there was a lot about this situation I hadn't thought through yet.

At the time, however, there was only one thing that made me stop in mid-sentence, and in retrospect, it was the least of our worries. What the heck was I supposed to call this girl? We already had one Jane Doe.

"Grace," Tori said, understanding my hesitation and filling in the gap. "We'll call her Grace."

"Why Grace?" I asked.

"Because once she was lost," Tori answered softly, "and now she's found."

Are you starting to understand why Tori is my best friend?

"What do you think?" I asked the dead girl. "Do you like the name Grace?"

The girl nodded. "It's pretty." Then she said uncertainly. "I think I was pretty once, too."

"Oh, honey," Tori said, "you still are. It's gonna be okay. We're gonna make this right for you."

Make it right? She was murdered and buried in an unmarked grave in the woods for thirty years. Is making that right even remotely possible? Probably not, but I was with Tori. We had to try for Grace—the same way we had to try for Jane. We were all they had now.

Chapter Twelve

The sun was so bright when we emerged from the trees, we stood at the edge of the forest blinking our eyes until our vision adjusted. Maybe it was the effect of the blinding light, but my brain kicked in with a lot of really important questions that should have already occurred to me.

I turned toward our spectral companion. "Grace," I asked, "why did you appear to us at the clearing this morning?"

"I heard you," she said. "You were louder than the others."

"The others?"

Grace nodded. "The people who walk on the trail," she answered. "When I hear them laughing and talking, I come to the edge of the trees and listen. If the people stay in the clearing a long time, I go over and try to make them hear me."

"But somehow Tori and I were different?"

She nodded. "Yes. You were shouting, so I came straight to the clearing."

Tori and I hadn't been shouting. In fact, on our walk up the mountain, we'd talked about how everyone else in town was probably still in church. We agreed that being on the mountain alone on such a beautiful, quiet day felt more like a sanctuary than any church we'd ever been to.

"We weren't shouting," I told Grace. "We were talking in our normal voice. What did you hear?"

The girl seemed to consider that. "You weren't shouting with your voices," she said hesitantly. "The pictures you saw in your head shouted."

She must have been referring to my vision. That's what she heard?

"Do you have any idea why you might have been able to hear what I saw?" I asked.

Grace nodded. "I think it was because when you fell you touched the place where that other girl was found," she said. "You know, the one people remember?"

Tori and I both shook our heads. Murdered, thrown away, and forgotten. Was it any wonder Grace's spirit wasn't at rest?

"Were you watching when they found her?" Tori asked.

"Yes," Grace said. "I hoped maybe if I went down there, the policemen would find me, too, but they didn't search far enough into the woods. Besides, I was still under the tree then so they couldn't have seen me anyway."

As much as I hated to ask her the next part, I didn't have much choice. She might be the only witness we'd ever find.

"Did you see who left the other girl on the trail?"

"No," Grace said, "but I felt him." A ripple went through her form, and Tori and I both shivered at the cold draft that washed over us in its wake. "He scared me," Grace continued. "It seemed like maybe I should know him."

She was still trembling, so I couched the next words with infinite care, "Do you think he was the same man who hurt you?"

A terrified look filled the hazy outlines of Grace's face, and she wavered in and out of sight. "I don't want to remember," she said. "Please don't make me remember."

"Hey," I soothed, "it's okay. I'm sorry. You don't have to remember. It's okay."

Grace was letting off little gasping sounds, but slowly her form stabilized.

"Better?" I asked.

She nodded.

"I need to ask you one more question," I said. "It's not scary, but it is important. Is that alright?"

"Yes," Grace said unsteadily. "I'll try."

I chose my words carefully. "Other than coming from the tree into the clearing," I asked, "have you ever tried to leave this place?"

Confusion washed over her face again, but she remained intact and visible.

"No. I'm not even sure I ever thought about leaving," she admitted. "It seemed like this was where I was supposed to be until somebody found me like they found that other girl."

Beside me, I felt Tori's hand on my arm. "Are you thinking about the others at the graveyard?" she whispered.

Grace didn't give me a chance to answer Tori. Instead, she blurted out all in a frightened rush, "I don't want to go to a graveyard! *Please* don't make me go to someplace like that."

I actually hadn't thought about taking Grace to the cemetery before that moment, but it wasn't a completely bad idea. Well, scratch that, at the moment it was a bad idea because she was so upset, but the company of other spirits, especially Jane, might help her.

Of course, there were two problems. The cemetery fence trapped the Briar Hollow ghosts. For all we knew, Grace wasn't going to be able to come with us at all if she was bound in a similar way to the forest.

If she *could* come with us, then the whole confinement thing must be tied to the cemetery. If we took her there, she might get trapped inside. That would be an awful thing to do to Grace, even if she would have company.

I watched as Tori assured the frightened spectre we had no intention of dumping her off at a graveyard. I could tell Tori and I were on the same page about the matter of Grace's mobility or lack thereof.

As soon as Tori was able to convince Grace that she would be staying with us, the girl brightened up—literally. It was almost as if the energy of the first excitement she felt in decades lent a new stability to her form. She appeared almost solid as she drifted eagerly ahead of us on the path.

"Are you thinking what I'm thinking?" Tori whispered when we were fairly certain we wouldn't be overheard.

"Yeah," I said. "This might be a really short trip for Grace if she runs into the kind of barrier that keeps the resident ghosts at the graveyard."

As it turns out, Grace's mobility improved by the minute. She floated to the parking lot where she waited patiently for us since she didn't know which car was mine. Even though we hadn't seen anyone on the trail, there were four other cars and a pickup in the small lot.

When I pointed to my candy-apple red Prius, Grace gasped. "Is *that* what you drive?"

"Yes," I said, smiling at her reaction. "It's a hybrid."

"What's a hybrid?" Grace asked, circling the car.

"Part of the time it runs on electricity stored in a battery in the trunk," I said. "It gets good gas mileage."

"Cool," Grace said. "I drove my Uncle Mike's old green Chevy Vega."

Okay. Now her situation was getting pathetic. The only car she drove before she died was a used Chevy Vega? Who has luck that bad?

Before I could unlock the doors, Grace was already sitting in the backseat waiting for us.

"Guess getting around isn't going to be an issue," Tori whispered. "She's totally up for a road trip."

"Yeah," I agreed, "but now we have another mystery. Why are the others under house arrest at the cemetery? Is it the unfinished business thing or is there more to the story?"

"Maybe because they have actual graves?" Tori suggested. "Maybe that keeps them tied to one spot."

"But what about ghosts that hang out in houses?" I asked. "They're not bound to their graves on a short leash."

"You got me," Tori said. "That's another question for the 'Ask Aunt Fiona' list."

I rolled my eyes. Aunt Fiona was not exactly proving to be a reliable—or for that matter an accessible—reference source.

When I got behind the wheel and pushed the start button, Grace leaned forward and stared at the digital dashboard. "Cool," she said again. "It looks like something off of *Star Trek*, but where's the cassette player?"

She definitely had some catching up to do.

We stopped at the store to drop Grace off before going to the Sheriff's Department to file a report. Technically, she could have come with us. In fact, from what I could tell, she could actually go anywhere she liked, but Grace proved to have something of an obedient streak.

Instinctively I knew that when she was alive, she was the kind of girl who never gave her mother any sort of trouble. That made it all the more difficult to understand how she wound up murdered and buried in a forest.

On the drive into town, when I suggested that Grace wait for us at the shop while we went to the Sheriff's office, she didn't protest. I think she was too grateful that we hadn't left her in the woods to risk being difficult.

I didn't voice my concern about having her ride shotgun on the trip to the Sheriff's Department because, frankly, it was a selfish concern on my part. I was afraid if she was involved in the process of "discovering" her own body, Grace would talk too much. To some degree, I'd have to answer her. I really wasn't ready to be branded as the new local nut job that talked to thin air.

Leaving Grace alone so soon after her earlier upset made me feel guilty, until she followed us upstairs and let out a happy squeal at the sight of my cats.

"Oh!" she exclaimed. "You have kitties. They're all so beautiful! What are their names?"

As she made a beeline for the cat-covered sofa, I identified the cast of players for her. The poor thing was clearly a fellow feline lover who had been deprived of furry companionship for too long. The girl sat down on the sofa, and just as Aunt Fiona had done two days earlier, Grace started petting Zeke with one hand while rubbing Yule's tummy with the other.

"You can touch them?" Tori asked in a shocked tone. "How does that work?"

"Cats aren't like other animals," Grace said as if she were intoning a principle law of the universe.

From the look Winston gave me, it was clear he thought I should know that already.

"So, you're going to be okay here by yourself?" I asked.

Grace looked at me and actually smiled. Then I realized what I'd said.

"Sorry," I said. "Guess you've got the alone thing down by now."

"Thank you for bringing me here," Grace said. "I'll be fine. I'm not by myself now."

She gazed adoringly into Zeke's eyes and I felt my throat constrict. I couldn't even imagine how alone this poor child had been for the last thirty years.

Grace saw me looking at her and misinterpreted my expression. "I won't bother anything," she said earnestly, "I promise."

"I'm not worried about that, honey," I said gently. I really wanted to go over to the sofa and give her a hug, but I think giving her four cats to pet probably meant more to her at that moment. "Make yourself at home," I said. "We'll be back as soon as we can."

Chapter Thirteen

Tori and I drove to the Sheriff's Department across the square even though we could have walked. I wanted to make sure we had our own transportation. After some initial confusion, the elderly dispatcher agreed to call the deputy, who was playing in a local softball league game.

He showed up in uniform, but not the right one. Even the most cash-strapped small-town sheriff doesn't have a Curly's Crispy Chicken sponsorship logo on the back of his shirts. The deputy listened and then disappeared into the back to change.

When he re-emerged, in the correct uniform, he explained he would have to pull the Sheriff out of a family reunion.

"Oh," I said, "I'm so sorry to interrupt his personal time."

"Don't be," the deputy said. "It's his wife's people. He'll be tickled pink."

The deputy told us to "get on back up to the trail" and to wait in the car until the local authorities arrived. "Now don't you all be going back up there to look at those bones again," he admonished through the open window of his cruiser.

"Don't worry about that," I assured him, and I meant it.

Tori and I sat in the lot for about fifteen minutes when the

Sheriff's car pulled up beside us. The deputy made perfunctory introductions, which the Sheriff cut off with a crisp, "Okay. Show us."

We dutifully led the way up the trail. No one said anything until we reached the clearing and started down toward the creek. The Sheriff stopped and stared pointedly at the "Stay On The Path" sign.

"I'm assuming you ladies can read?" he said gravely.

"That's my fault, sir," Tori said quickly. "I really wanted to win that photo contest I was telling you about."

"Uh-huh," the Sheriff grunted noncommittally. "All right. Go on."

With me in the lead, we retraced our steps to the decaying hickory. I pointed to the trunk and said, "The skeleton is in there."

Unclipping a MagLite from his belt, the Sheriff circled the tree, then leaned down and shined the light inside. He stayed in that position for a minute or two before straightening and pushing his hat back on his head. "Okay. You want to take me through exactly how you managed to spot a skull back in there?"

Tori's demonstration was an Oscar-worthy performance. She produced her first "mushroom" photograph, all the while boring the socks off both men as she rattled on about how and when to use a fill flash. She even pulled up the current spate of "Signs of Decay" entries on her phone and showed the contest site first to the Sheriff and then to the deputy. By the time she was done, they were both more than ready to believe our story to get her to shut up.

From there, the legal process took over. The Sheriff called the State Police for backup and told us to go back to the clearing and wait to give our statements. A quartet of burly State Troopers arrived in less than thirty minutes. They separated us to take our statements and then told us we were free to go.

As we were starting to walk away, I called out to the Sheriff. He excused himself and left the troopers talking to a newly arrived team of crime scene techs.

"What can I do for you, Miss Hamilton?" the Sheriff asked.

"I wondered if you could let us know what you find out about those bones," I said. "I mean if that's not against procedure or something."

The Sheriff was a big man and vaguely stereotypical in that famous Southern sheriff way. He seemed to have made up his mind that Tori and I weren't criminals because his earlier genial good humor now replaced his earlier brusqueness.

In response to my question, the Sheriff rolled his omnipresent toothpick over to the other side of his mouth and said, "Miss Hamilton, in a town like Briar Hollow, there's no keeping anything secret. I knew you moved into Fiona's shop with four tomcats before you even got their litter boxes filled. I was sorry about her passing."

That was a good sign. He knew my aunt and apparently liked her.

"Thank you," I said, "and my name is Jinx. You have a point about small town . . . information sharing."

"The word you're looking for is gossip," he grinned.

"How did you know my aunt?" I asked.

"Everyone knows everyone else in Briar Hollow," he said, "but I played dominoes with Fiona at the VFW Hall on Friday nights. My name is John, by the way," he finished, offering me his hand.

John Johnson? Seriously?

"I know," he said, reading my reaction as we shook hands. "My folks didn't have much imagination in the naming department."

I glanced left and right and then said in a stage whisper, "Don't tell anyone, but my real name is Norma Jean."

Sheriff John let out a belly laugh. "Don't worry," he said. "Your secret is safe with me. I'll come by the shop and let you know if we find out anything."

I thanked him and then said, "Uh, John, isn't this the place where the local Jane Doe was found in 1995?"

The Sheriff looked at me appraisingly. "How do you know about her?"

"I found a file of clippings about the case in my aunt's shop," I answered truthfully. "It looked like Aunt Fiona had an interest in the case."

John pushed his hat back again and let out a puff of air. "That she did," he said. "Fiona blamed herself for not getting that gal's name when she was in her shop."

Tori cleared her throat, and the Sheriff looked at her questioningly.

"Isn't it kind of . . . well . . . more than a coincidence that there's another body pretty much in the same spot that other girl was found?" Tori asked.

"Who are you again?" the Sheriff asked.

"Tori Andrews," she said. "I'm Jinx's best friend. I've been helping her get settled in."

"You watch a lot of those CSI-like crime shows and such?" the Sheriff asked.

I knew for a fact that Tori hated those shows, but she had sense enough to play dumb and to play along. "Yes, sir," she said feigning sheepish embarrassment. "I do."

"Well, don't get it in your head this is anything like one of those programs," he said firmly. "That skeleton probably belongs to some drifter who climbed in there to get warm and died."

Uh-huh. That was small-town-sheriff speak for, "I think we've got a serial killer on our hands, but I'm not about to say so." We pretended to buy his explanation and left.

On the drive back to town, Tori was strangely quiet.

"Okay," I said. "What's going on in that head of yours?"

Out of nowhere, she said, "I think I need to ask Tom for some time off."

"To do what?"

"Help you get really settled at the store and solve these murders."

Somehow, I think she reversed the order of importance there, but I let it slide.

"You can't ask Tom for more time off right after I up and quit on him. He'll flip out."

Tori stared out the window for a minute and then said, "Maybe I wouldn't mind if he did flip out."

I recognized her tone of voice. It was the same one she used with sentences that began, "Hey, Jinksy, I've been thinking…" Those scenarios ended with me jumping out of an airplane or something equally insane because "it will be fun."

"Are you trying to get yourself fired?" I asked even though I could guess where this was going.

She turned to look at me. "You need help," she said again.

"Those girls aren't going to get any deader in the next week," I said. "Come back next weekend."

Tori sighed. "Okay. I guess I'm going to have to walk you through this step by step. You need to hire me to work in the store with you. Since I'm going to be living in a room out back, you don't have to pay me much."

"There's no room out back of the store," I said, frowning.

Did I mention I can be ridiculously literal at times?

With infinite patience, Tori said, "There will be a room when we have it built, which I will help pay for. There's plenty of space between the back door and the alley."

No, Tori is not the pushiest woman on the planet. We've

been talking about running a business together since we opened our first lemonade stand at age six. The plan changed a lot over the years. We envisioned ourselves as everything from bookstore owners to furniture refinishers. (The last idea went by the wayside fast. Too brutal on the nails.)

In that weird, Vulcan-BFF-mind-meld thing we do, Tori read my thoughts.

"The shop pulls every idea we've ever had under one roof," she said excitedly. "Myrtle makes it all a jillion times better than we could have imagined. If we start carrying a few books and put in an espresso bar, people will start coming in to hang out. Remember how Chase talked about all those local musicians? We could have live music nights and . . ."

While she talked, I started thinking. The news that Aunt Fiona left me the store made me apprehensive about becoming a storekeeper, but I'm a fast study. Then I realized I was, theoretically, in charge of a store with a mind of its own. So far Myrtle was cheerful and helpful, but what if that changed?

Then there was the witch thing. In the last three days, I'd gone from talking to my cats to moving objects with my mind and asking stray ghosts to come home with me. As long as Tori and I kept up our constant running chatter of clever jokes and bright ideas, I was fine.

I hadn't bothered to mention waking up three times the night before from heart-pounding nightmares, all with scenarios where my newfound magic went horribly wrong and hurt the people I love. Even with drastically changed circumstances, I continued to follow my original plan—faking confidence on every front.

Tori finally noticed I wasn't saying anything. With a worried note of doubt, she asked. "Don't you think it's a good idea? I mean, I kind of thought you would have come up with it yourself by now."

Which I should have. #BestFriendFail

"Which good idea?" I asked, intentionally flashing her both a big grin and an apology with my eyes. "You've spit out about six dozen so far. I'm sorry, Tori. There's been too much going on for me to think straight, which is what I have you for."

When I saw the incredible relief on her features, I felt even worse for making her think even for an instant that I had given up on our long-held entrepreneurial dreams.

"That's okay, Jinksy. I know you've been on overload. So, first, I tell Tom I quit, and then we hire a contractor."

I laughed. "Okay. Plan revision time. You have to give Tom at least a month's notice. He hired us right out of high school, and he's been a good boss even if he does holler all the time. We can't both quit on him."

Blowing out a sigh, Tori said, "You're right. Man, it sucks to be a grown-up."

"Agreed," I said. "But seriously, it'll take at least a month to get that room added on. You have to go back to your place so you can be in at 5:30 a.m. on the dot for the six o'clock breakfast run. I can hold down the fort until you get back next weekend. It's not like we don't talk, text, email, and Facetime every day. You won't miss anything good, I promise. Besides, you have to tell your mom about this plan."

Tori's face fell. "I thought maybe you'd tell her."

"Oh, *hell* no," I said emphatically. "I'm still recovering from the fit my mom threw when I told her I was moving to Briar Hollow. You're on your own with Gemma."

"Coward," she accused.

"Guilty," I confessed.

"But overall, we have a plan, right?" Tori asked.

I took my right hand off the wheel and held out my fist. We did a celebratory bump. It was a plan, one forged as I pulled up in front of the shop and spied Grace through the big display window.

"Huh," I said, as I got out of the car, "Grace is downstairs."

The instant I unlocked the door, Grace said, all in a guilty rush, "The cats are safe upstairs. I didn't open any doors or anything."

See what I mean? So *not* a wild child.

"I wasn't worried," I assured her. "Did you decide to have a look around?"

"Myrtle asked me if I wanted to come down and talk to her," Grace said happily. "This place is great!"

"Oh my God!" Tori gasped. "Myrtle talked to you . . . *is* talking to you? Have you seen her? What does she look like? Is she a ghost?"

The shop laughed and Grace joined in. "Myrtle says you ask too many questions all at once. She says she's not a ghost."

"Then what is she?" I asked.

"She's the store," Grace said matter-of-factly. Then she shifted into a more complicated gear. "So now that you've told the police about my skeleton, can we call my mom? Please?"

Chapter Fourteen

It took us the better part of an hour to make Grace understand the police couldn't ID her skeletal remains without running tests and plugging the results into the missing person's database. Then she hit us with a question we couldn't field. "What if no one reported me missing?"

"Well," I said, "that might make it harder, but we'll still figure out who you are."

Yeah, I know. I walked out on a limb. You try denying a 30-year-old ghost who wants to talk to her mother.

Tori had thrown her stuff into a bag and prepared to take off. We said our goodbyes out front on the sidewalk.

"You gonna be okay?" she whispered in my ear when we hugged.

"Yeah," I said, "but I'm already looking forward to Friday."

When I went back inside, Grace floated around peering into the display cases. "Hey," I said, "I'm really beat. I'm going to go to bed. Do you . . . uh . . . need anything?"

"No," Grace said. "I'm fine. I'll just stay here and talk to Myrtle. I don't want to keep you up."

Obedient and considerate. This was my idea of the perfect houseguest.

I immediately fell asleep, worn out from the weekend's activities. The cats woke me up the next morning promptly at five o'clock. They apparently didn't intend to change their schedule to accommodate me.

While I drank my coffee, I made a list of things to accomplish for the day, including going next door to "say hi" to Amity. I wanted to get a better look at her shop. I didn't want to stock anything that would put me in direct competition with her. I thought she mainly sold regional pottery and paintings, but I needed to make sure before I began talking with local craftsmen.

I also wanted to ask Chase if he could recommend a contractor to discuss the addition to the back of the store. Tori sent a long email describing what she had in mind. The major points were: galley kitchen, Murphy bed, and "awesome" shower. She currently lived in less than 400 square feet. We could make this work.

Grace stood at the front of the shop looking out the window when I came down. "Good morning," I said. "How are you?"

"Good," she said. "There's so much more to see here than up in the woods. Can I go upstairs and be with the cats?"

"Of course you can," I said. "Would you like me to turn the TV set on for you?"

"Oh!" she said. "Is *All My Children* still on?"

"Sorry, it was canceled."

Grace gasped. "They canceled Erica? Who was she married to when the story quit?"

I winced. "I honestly don't know."

"Well, what about *One Life to Live*?"

"Also gone."

"*General Hospital*?"

"That one is still on," I said, "but not until this afternoon."

"Oh, okay," Grace said. "I forgot about time being important. I'll go see the cats now."

And like that, she was gone.

"Myrtle," I said, "take care of her."

The lights dimmed and came back up as if the store had just nodded. Good enough for me. I went out the front door, locking it behind me, and greeted Festus, who was sunning on his bench.

"Good morning, you old con artist," I said, scratching his ears. "Your dad ratted you out. I know about the zoomies."

Festus ignored me, choosing instead to fix the courthouse with his thousand-yard stare. For the uninitiated, that's the feline version of pleading the Fifth.

Chase was at his workbench behind the counter when I walked in. "Good morning," I said brightly. "Ready to tackle a new week?"

"Well, hi!" he greeted me, putting down his tools and wiping his hands as he stood up. "You're up bright and early."

"I have a question," I said. "Do you know a good local contractor?"

"I do," he said. "Mark Haskell is the best in the county. Are you going to do some remodeling?"

"Kind of," I said, filling him in on the plan for Tori to join the business.

"What a great idea," Chase said. "She's right, there's plenty of room back there. Mark did a similar job on the other side of the square last year. Remember the pizza guy? He lives behind his shop, too. I'm sure he'd let you and Tori see his place if you ask. Mark told me there's all kind of great space-saving ideas worked into the design. I'll introduce you if you like."

"I would like that."

"We could go over there for supper one night this week," Chase said. "He has pasta dishes at night."

For a minute the smooth transition to a dinner invitation left me speechless. When I didn't answer, he said, "I mean, if you like pasta."

"Pasta. I do. Like it. Pasta, I mean," I babbled. "Uh, yes, thank you. Just, uh, let me know when."

Chase grinned. "It's a date."

A date. There it was. He used the word. Date. But it wasn't a date date. It was more like a date—as in a day on the calendar—with a number. Right? Jinx, get ahold of yourself.

"Right," I said, a shade too brightly. "It's a date. Okay. Well, I'll let you get back to work. I need to go see Amity. I'll . . . talk to you later. . ."

Chase grinned at me all the way out the door. I hoped that was because he thought I was cute, not because I sounded like a raving idiot.

As I came out the door, Festus gave me a pointed, "Meowrr."

"Hush, you," I said under my breath. "Keep your opinions to yourself."

My visit with Amity was considerably less eventful but equally satisfying. Although she billed her shop as "local crafts," it was really an art gallery that also carried pottery and a few sculptures. None of the inventory I was considering would compete with her wares. When I told her I was considering putting in an espresso bar and having live music on occasion, she grew more excited by the minute.

"Fan-tas-tic," she enthused. A word she then repeated several times, varying the emphasis on the syllables until she sounded like she was chanting some kind of New Age mantra.

"We could do event nights," she said. "The customers could drink wine and try to draw with me, and drink coffee and listen to music with you."

As Amity expressed it, the concept was amorphously free-form, but I got the gist of the concept. If several of the businesses on the street stayed open the same night, we would all benefit from the evening traffic. I couldn't wait to share *that* idea with Tori. We could really be onto something here!

I managed to extricate myself from Amity around nine o'clock, so I was only a few minutes late turning the orange-and-black sign in the front window from "Closed" to "Open." For a brief ten minutes, I felt in control of the retail thing. Then my first customer did his best to knock the wind out of my sails.

An elderly gentleman marched in the front door and approached the counter with a commanding demeanor. I fought the urge to step back. "I'm here for my regular order," he announced, and stood there and glared.

No name.

No clue what that order might be.

Not one thing to help me do my job.

I sensed his mounting impatience.

Mustering my best, the-customer-is always-right face, I said, "I'm so sorry, sir. You may have heard that my aunt, Fiona Ryan, passed away last week. She left me the store, and this is my first day. Would you mind telling me your name and giving me an idea of what I'm looking for?"

"I do mind," the old coot snapped.

Gritting my teeth to keep my smile in place, I said, "Well, sir, if I don't know your name, how can I look for your order?"

"She never knew my name and she figured it out," he said. "Improvise."

Great.

"Let me look in the back," I said, excusing myself to the relative privacy of the storeroom.

Glancing over my shoulder to make sure my irascible

customer hadn't followed me, I whispered urgently, "Okay, Myrtle, sorry to bother you, but what does this guy want?"

Surprisingly, Rodney answered me. The rat came out and trotted over to a small brown bag lined up with several others on a shelf in the corner. I peered at the bag. In Aunt Fiona's neat handwriting, the label read, "Monday, 9:30 a.m." I glanced at my watch. 9:35. This had to be the man's order.

Curious, I gently opened the bag, careful not to wrinkle the paper, and drew out a *Ziplock* bag full of some green plant neatly chopped . . . oh God . . . was Aunt Fiona selling pot to the locals? Then I saw the second tag, which read "horny goat weed" and gave instructions for steeping tea.

From the front of the store, the old guy barked, "I don't have all day, young woman."

Returning the *Ziplock* bag to the discreet confines of its brown outer wrapper, I returned to the counter and made my first sale. Thankfully Aunt Fiona wrote the price on the bag. The old man left without thanking me or acknowledging my less than heartfelt "have a good day." He slammed the door so hard the pane rattled.

As I watched the man stomp across Main Street without looking right or left, oblivious to the cars screeching to a stop to avoid hitting him, I took out my phone and looked up horny goat weed.

Squinting to make out the tiny words on the screen, I read, "According to folklore, horny goat weed's reputed aphrodisiac qualities . . ."

Whoa!

Too. Much. Information.

I hastily closed the browser. I needed brain bleach to get the image of that old guy . . .

La la la la la la la.

Since Rodney did me a solid, I cut a slice of the apple I planned to have a sandwich for lunch and went into the storeroom. When I called, my new rodent sidekick came out and gratefully accepted the treat.

"You saved me, little man," I said, lightly scratching the bridge of his nose. I giggled when he wiggled his whiskers and scrunched up his face with pleasure. "I don't suppose you know where Fiona kept a list of her regular orders?"

Without hesitation, the rat carefully put the apple slice down, trotted the length of the shelf, and executed a perfect jump to the top of the wooden file cabinet. He leaned over the edge, patted the top drawer with his paw, and gave me a look that said, "You getting this?"

I went over and opened the drawer. To my surprise, when I leaned to look inside, Rodney jumped on my shoulder and lightly held on to my blouse as he, too, peered into the drawer and waved a directional paw.

"Okay, okay," I said, "hold your horses, Rodney."

I thumbed through the folders, and sure enough, the third one back read, "Standing Herb Orders." The list included phone numbers for suppliers. I cross-referenced the list against the rows of brown paper bags on the corner shelf. I would have everything covered until Grandpa Stud Muffin came back next Monday.

With Rodney's help, I checked the shelves, figured out which herbs needed to be restocked, and called the appropriate outlets. Everyone I talked to was serenely Zen in a way that suggested at least some of them used herbal products they *didn't* list in their catalogs. I honestly don't remember ever saying "namaste" before that morning, but by noon I'd uttered the word at least two dozen times.

When Rodney tugged on my blouse and nodded toward his cage, I was actually sorry to let the rat down from my shoulder. To show my appreciation, I gave him a second apple slice. "Sorry if I wore you out, little guy," I said, as the rat trotted off with his reward.

To his credit, Rodney gallantly looked back over his shoulder as if to say "don't mention it," before going home for what I assumed would be a well-earned midday snooze.

The rest of the day passed quietly. A couple of people dropped by just to say hello and to offer me their condolences. A tourist couple came in at three o'clock and waxed rhapsodic about the "rustic charm" of the shop. I suspected they were eyeing my wares for resale on eBay, but they left empty-handed.

I spent plenty of time thinking about having dinner with Chase McGregor that night. We agreed via text message to meet out front about six o'clock for the walk across the square. I planned to close at five, so I'd have enough time to check on Grace, who had been absent all day, feed the cats, and freshen up.

That's girl speak for "obsess about what I was going to wear."

Which was silly, since I looked perfectly fine to go to the local pizzeria with my next-door neighbor/business acquaintance. Except that Chase had already edged over into the next-door neighbor/friend category and had the potential for a complete re-classification.

There was one problem that had me chewing the inside of my lip with worry.

My re-classifications of male acquaintances rarely went well.

Chapter Fifteen

Now for the brief and depressing history of my love life.

Unlike Tori, I don't have a preference for mildly "bad" boys. Please don't take that as disloyalty. Her standards are "tattoos must be correctly spelled." Tori freely admits none of her exes know the difference between Mensa and Mentos.

After graduation, Tori and I both stayed with our high school sweethearts through that first summer. By the fall, however, mine went off to college. Hers got a nickel in the state pen for believing his buddy Luther when he said, "Sit in the car and wait for me while I pop into this liquor store. Oh, and dude, keep the car running."

My boyfriend, Billy Wayne, loved *Star Wars* and his engineering textbooks more than me, or really, more than anything in life. He could spot excruciatingly detailed mistakes in a Boba Fett costume at ComiCon but couldn't remember my birthday to save his life.

Like many high school couples before us, college doomed our future, mainly because he actually went to college, and I stayed in my tiny hometown.

Unlike Billy Wayne, our class valedictorian, I put in an average high school performance. No scholarships for me. My folks couldn't afford to send me to college. I could have applied for student loans and probably gotten them. But I couldn't see how going into years of debt would make my life better, especially since I didn't have a clue what I wanted to do.

Billy Wayne took to college like the proverbial duck to water. I don't imagine he ever achieved true popularity, but he found droves of fellow *Star Wars* nerds in the engineering department. Ultimately, he married one of them. She dressed as Princess Lei for the ceremony, complete with cinnamon bun hair extensions on either side of her head.

Tori and I spent that first winter not dating. We enjoyed numerous "men are worthless jerks" conversations over junk food and chick flicks. Then she met Cody, and I started seeing Jesse.

We've never had any best friend chick drama over guys, but Cody and Jesse were the exceptions. I couldn't stand Cody; Tori couldn't stand Jesse. We aired our viewpoints in a series of wholly uncharacteristic catfights.

The situation finally escalated to the point that we dumped both guys in a show of solidarity. We might have been without boyfriends, but we had our friendship back. We both apologized over several bottles of commiseration wine, and once again, swore off men.

For the most part, I meant it. Other than a few dinners and an occasional concert or something, none of the guys who asked me out stayed on my radar. Tori, on the other hand, went through quite the who's who of available manhood. Thankfully, none of them tried to put a ring on it, because none of them were, in my opinion, good enough for her.

By the time I inherited the shop, I hadn't been on a date for at least a year, maybe two. The last such social engagement never made it past the first layer of brain cells and into deep memory. I think we went for fried chicken, but I can't be certain. I couldn't tell you his name to save my life.

The prospect of dinner with Chase excited me because we genuinely seemed to have a lot in common.

I shared all of this with Grace in a highly encapsulated form as I feverishly changed tops looking for the perfect outfit. Grace was the only other female present to offer an opinion on my clothing choices.

"That one kinda makes you look like someone's grandma," she said, as politely as possible, when I emerged in a sale rack blouse with a ruffly collar.

Even if her fashion sense was arguably thirty years old, I agreed with her.

"Why don't you wear a solid top and keep your jeans on," she said. "You look good for a woman your age."

A woman my age?

"How old do you think I am?" I asked indignantly.

"I don't know. Maybe 25 or something?" Grace asked. She floated cross-legged over the foot of my bed watching me stare at myself in the mirror for the umpteenth time.

Since she made me four years younger than I actually was, I forgave her.

"Close enough." I said. "And thanks about the jeans, I think."

Truth be told, she was right. When in doubt, simplify. I picked out a navy top with a V-neck, kept my jeans on, and at the last minute remembered to change out of running shoes in favor of sandals. (When you're a waitress, comfortable shoes trump fashion.)

"So, what do you think?" I asked.

"You look nice," Grace said. "Just right for going out for pizza."

"Will you be okay here if I leave the TV on for you and the cats?"

"Oh, sure," she said. "I'm fine." Then she added, shyly, "You'll come back and tell me all about your date, right?"

The way she said it made me realize she seemed sadder than she'd been when we first found her in the woods.

"Grace, honey," I said, "are you sure you're okay?"

Her form faded in and out as if she was uncertain how to answer. "I'm realizing how much . . . life . . . I've missed," she finally said.

Being dead will do that to a person.

"I'm sorry," I said. "Is it harder being here?"

"Oh, no," she said, "please don't make me go back."

"I'm not going to make you go back," I said. "I'm worried about you."

"Oh," she said again, "thank you. I . . . I think I might be missing my girlfriends."

Now, that could mean progress.

"Have you remembered something about your life?" I asked.

"Not really," she said. "When you were trying on clothes, it felt like I did that before and had fun. Or at least I think that's what I was remembering. It felt like I might have been happy."

Our roles should have been reversed. She should have been the one getting ready for a date. It broke my heart that I couldn't fix that, but as awful as this will sound, dead really is dead.

Chapter Sixteen

When I stepped onto the sidewalk, Chase was sitting on the bench by the front door, dressed in a maroon polo and softly worn jeans, with his hair still damp from the shower. The instant he saw me, he jumped to his feet, a smile spreading across his face.

"Hi!" he said. "You look nice."

I returned the smile and thanked him for the compliment. My eyes fell on the stack of books sitting on the bench. "Wow," I said. "Do we need a wheelbarrow for those?"

Chase laughed. "No, I think I can manage."

"Let me take some," I offered, holding out my hands.

"You sure?" he said, reaching for the books.

Was I sure? Of course, I was sure. I wanted to know what he was reading.

"Absolutely," I said. "I'll consider it pre-pasta exercise."

Chase selected the lighter volumes and handed them to me, holding the heftier books with both hands as we started walking toward the library. When he passed the books to me, I quickly read two titles: *Regiments and Uniforms of the Civil War* and *Civil War Collector's Encyclopedia.*

"Is the war about to break out again?" I asked.

"Huh?" Chase said, crinkling his forehead. Then the source of my question dawned on him. "Oh, no. I've been commissioned to make boots for a Civil War movie that's going to be shot in Pennsylvania. The director wants everything authentic down to the last stitch."

He held up a copy of *Crimson Shore* by Douglas Preston and Lincoln Child. "This is more my speed for pleasure reading."

My eyes lit up. "Have you read the whole series?" I asked excitedly. "Which one was your favorite? I was completely hooked after I read *Cabinet of Curiosities*."

Chase looked shocked. "You read the Pendergast books?"

I nodded. "I loved the one about Helen."

"*Cold Vengeance*," Chase said. "Could you believe the bit with the lion?"

We returned the books and continued our animated conversation all the way to the Stone Hearth. The one-man pizzeria became my new happy place the instant I walked in the door.

The restaurant occupied what must have been an old general store. The building looked older than mine and benefited from a loving restoration. The hardwood floors dipped and rolled from years of wear, but also gleamed with a new hand-rubbed finish.

The bare stone walls presented diners with a fascinating interplay of textures and shapes to study while they waited. The smell of cooking pizza wafted throughout the space from the open-hearth oven visible in the kitchen. The evening was warm, but the cavernous interior of the restaurant created a cool oasis.

The proprietor, introduced to me as "Pete, the pizza guy," took our order and brought us a carafe of red wine. Chase and I segued from books to films. When our food came, we had discovered a shared love of long bike rides.

As I took the first bite of absolutely heavenly lasagna, Chase said, "So, when were you going to tell me?"

"Tell you what?"

"That you and Tori went up to Weber's Gap yesterday and found a skeleton."

"Oh," I said, reaching for my wine as a stalling tactic. "That."

With the previous owner of that skeleton camped out on my sofa binge watching *Gilmore Girls* on my laptop, I forgot the discovery of the remains likely caused a stir in town.

"Oh, *that*?" Chase said, arching his eyebrows. "Have you looked at the news today?"

I shook my head. "No, I really don't watch the news. It's too scary and depressing."

"But how will you know when something major happens in the world?"

"I get a text from Tori," I answered honestly. "Seriously, I wouldn't have known about 9/11 for hours if she hadn't called me that morning."

Chase took a drink of his wine. "Well, your approach probably makes for a happier life, but I have to admit I'm an information junkie. Your discovery up at the Gap made the news in Winston-Salem."

"You're kidding," I said, "was it a slow news day or something?"

"You really don't keep up, do you?" Chase said. "There was another skeleton found on a hiking trail about an hour from here last month."

A tingling sensation started up my spine. I didn't know if the feeling was my newfound magic or my trusty old Spidey sense saying loud and clear, *"Uh oh."*

What I said was, "Really? Have the police identified the body?"

At that moment Pete arrived with a warm loaf of bread.

Chase and I both tore off fragrant chunks and dipped them in the bowl of olive oil our host also deposited on the table. Chase didn't answer my question until we were alone again.

"All the police have been able to determine is that those remains are about twenty-five years old, and they belong to a young girl."

I ran the numbers in my head. The last thing Grace remembered happened thirty years ago. Now remains that had been out in the woods twenty-five years turned up. Jane was found twenty years ago. Coincidence or pattern?

Fortunately, my brain and my mouth can run in different directions with a fair amount of efficiency. "That's awful," I heard myself say. "Do the police think there's a connection to the remains we found?"

"They aren't saying anything official right now," Chase replied. "But, of course, the reporters are having a field day with the two discoveries. I'm surprised they haven't shown up on your doorstep."

Which they probably would. I needed to check the news stories and call Tori later. I hadn't heard from her which was strange. Normally she would let me know if we made the news. Especially since that never happened to us before.

"So," Chase prodded, "how *did* you find the skeleton?"

I gave Chase a slightly sanitized version of the previous day's events. I went with the "it was a pretty day, so we decided to get outdoors" angle. The story made sense because we spent Saturday cooped up in the shop. I ended with a faithful recitation of the photo contest alibi. Never vary the major details of a concocted story.

Thankfully, the conversation wandered off to a discussion of photography and cameras, an interest Chase shared with Tori. No more talk of skeletal remains and potential serial killers—which suited me. Neither topic qualified as first "getting to know you" material.

When the dinner crowd thinned out, Pete showed us his apartment, which was almost exactly what Tori wanted. The well-ordered space included so many clever storage ideas, I was shocked to learn Pete lived in 375 square feet. He suggested I bring Tori over on Saturday.

"She'll drive you nuts with questions," I warned.

"That's okay," Pete said. "I don't mind. Small spaces demand advance planning. Besides, your friend sounds like fun."

I already noted the lack of a wedding ring on Pete's left hand. Chase said the pizzeria was a one-man operation. I know, I know. Stop playing matchmaker. But let's be honest. With Tori's track record, Pete would be a breath of fresh air.

When we exited the restaurant, the streetlights bathed the courthouse square in pools of yellow light. "Would you do me the honor of a stroll, Miss Hamilton?" Chase said, affecting a courtly Southern accent and offering me his arm.

Shifting instantly into Scarlett mode, I said, "Why, Mr. McGregor, I would be delighted."

When I slipped my hand into the crook of Chase's arm, I felt pleasantly hard muscle beneath my fingers. Could a guy get that buff working on shoes?

"How long have you been a cobbler?" I asked.

"Since I was twenty," Chase said. "About ten years. Thank you for using the right word for what I do. I get really tired of being introduced as the 'shoe repair guy.'"

I shuddered. "Ugh. I don't blame you. Cobbler is a wonderful, old-fashioned word."

"Which most people think refers to a gooey fruit dessert with lots of crust."

"Also a wonderful thing."

Chase chuckled and said, "Peach."

I responded with, "Cherry."

This was a good sign. We were already probing deeper into

each other's likes and dislikes. Although my "starting a relationship" gears suffered from rust the evening seemed to be moving along nicely.

Chase didn't slow his steps when we passed by our shops. About halfway to the grocery store on the corner, he said, "I'm sorry. I didn't ask if you'd like to go around again."

"Sure," I said. "It's a beautiful night, and I'm having a wonderful time."

"Me, too," he said. "I'm sorry about the reason why you moved in next door, but I'm really glad you did."

"Thank you," I said, "but I'm sorry about the reason, too."

"Do you miss her?"

I sighed. "Truthfully, I hadn't seen Aunt Fiona much in the last few years. She and my mom had a dicey relationship. Fiona and I did talk on the phone fairly often though. I loved knowing she and the shop were here when I needed them."

"Isn't that funny," Chase said thoughtfully. "People always mention Fiona and the shop in the same breath. It's almost like the shop was a second person."

"Well," I said, going for a neutral comment, "you have to admit the place has personality."

Actually, Myrtle was loaded with personality, but I couldn't explain *that* to Chase.

"Fiona sorta treated the place like it was a person," he said.

That warning bell sounded in my head again. Fiona didn't leave me with a copy of *How to Be a Witch for Dummies*, but I instinctively knew this was information best shared selectively.

"Why do you say that?" I asked innocently.

Chase hesitated. "I don't want to make it sound like Fiona was getting senile or anything, but she did talk to herself a lot."

"Did she?" I asked.

"She really did," Chase affirmed. "Sometimes when she couldn't find something, she'd ask the shop to show her where it was."

God, Fiona. Did you even know the meaning of the word "discretion"?

"You're not going to offend me by saying Aunt Fiona was eccentric," I assured him. "In our family, she's known as Crazy Aunt Fiona."

"Fiona wasn't crazy," Chase said loyally, "but she was different."

Now there was one for the Understatement Hall of Fame.

Even though our conversation was still going strong, I halted in front of our stores after the third circuit of the square. I couldn't tell Chase I felt guilty about leaving Grace and the cats alone. The ghost might not mind, but the cats were a different matter.

As we said our goodnights, Chase leaned in and gave me a soft kiss on the lips. He wasn't making a move, so much as testing the waters to see if we were headed in the same direction. I think we passed the test.

He waited until I was safely inside to turn toward his shop. As I closed the door, I heard him say, "Good night, Jinx. Remember, knock on the pipes if you need anything."

No sooner did I lock the door than I heard Tony Orlando and Dawn singing, *"Knock three times on the ceiling if you want me . . ."*

"Very funny, Myrtle," I said to the darkened store. "Quit spying on me and start listening to some new music."

The store rewarded me with a few bars of *Single Ladies.*

Note to self. Never underestimate Myrtle.

Chapter Seventeen

I found Grace and the cats were on the sofa right where I left them. As promised, I filled my ectoplasmic houseguest in on the details of my date before excusing myself to call Tori—who wanted the same details but interrupted me way more.

When I finally got a word in edgewise, I asked, "So is Chase right? Were we on the news?"

"We were on the news in that a talking head identified us as 'hikers who disobeyed the signs and wandered off the path,'" Tori said.

I didn't have to be looking at her to know she rolled her eyes.

"Did you know about the other girl who was found a month ago?" I asked.

"I remember hearing the story," Tori said, "but I didn't pay much attention to it. Are you thinking what I'm thinking?"

"Oh, I don't know," I said sarcastically. "Three murdered girls in a radius of fifty miles, all estimated to have been killed five years apart? Let me go out on a limb here. Pattern?"

Tori laughed, bitterly. "Exactly. Has Grace remembered

anything? She could have been the first victim."

"No," I said, lowering my voice. "But, she thinks she led a happy life."

Tori groaned. "God, could this get any sadder?"

I really, really hoped not.

Glancing at the clock, I said, "You have to be up for the breakfast shift. We better hang up. I'm going to spend some time on the Internet tomorrow seeing what I can find out about missing persons in the area for the last thirty years. Let's Facetime when you get off work."

"That sounds like a plan," she said, "but before I let you go, I gave Tom my 30-day notice."

"How did he take it?"

"Oh, he banged a skillet and called me an ingrate," Tori said, "and then muttered something about how he'd been waiting for me to tag along after you."

"Which in Tom-speak means he was expecting this and wasn't really mad, he just had to put on a show."

"Exactly," Tori said. "He's already got three girls lined up. He wants me to be there when he talks to them since I will also be expected to train them."

"Train them?" I said. "Haven't any of them waited tables before?"

"They all have," Tori said. "I'm supposed to teach them how he likes things done."

That made me laugh. There's no mystery about how Tom likes things done. He bellows his preferences at the top of his lungs all day, every day.

"Lucky you."

"Maybe I can save them the case of nerves his hollering gives people until they figure out he wouldn't hurt a fly," she sighed. "Selective deafness is an important job skill when you work for Tom."

We said our goodnights, and I went into the living room to

shut off the laptop. Grace excused herself to go talk to Myrtle. The cats watched her disappear through the door (literally *through* the door) and then turned accusatory eyes on me.

"I know, I know," I said. "I should be the one sitting with you on the sofa for hours on end. Kinda trying to have a life here guys. Grace doesn't have that problem."

That won me four diffident and resigned feline expressions that softened marginally as we trouped to the bedroom. I would like to tell you that I am in charge of the allocation of mattress-based real estate. But that would be a lie. The system works like this. They pick their spots. I take what's left over—six inches on the edge of the bed.

When started to drift off, a sound in my bedroom brought me instantly awake. Sitting up carefully so as not to awaken my furry bedmates, I called out softly, "Grace, is that you?"

When there was no answer, I turned on the bedside lamp. An empty wine bottle floated at the foot of my bed with a rolled-up piece of paper inside.

Only one person I knew could be that theatrical. Aunt Fiona.

I drew the bottle toward me with my newfound magic. The cork popped out and the bottle upended itself, allowing the note to slide neatly through the neck. As the paper landed in my lap, the bottle righted itself and politely went to sit on the bedside table without being asked.

I unrolled the message and found several lines penned in Aunt Fiona's neat script. "Jinx," it began, "would you please quit hollering at me all the time? I can't come to the shop right now."

Right. Because being dead involves a non-stop round of appointments that won't wait?

"You're doing great, honey," she continued. "I'm so glad you've been in touch with Colonel Longworth and the other spirits at the cemetery. It was one of my greatest disappointments that I was never able to discover Jane's real name. I didn't know that Grace was up there on the trail."

Geez. Was Aunt Fiona watching me through some kind of metaphysical nanny cam or was Myrtle a big snitch?

And, what did the wording of that sentence mean anyway?

Did Aunt Fiona really *not* know there was a second ghost of a murdered girl, or was she saying she hadn't known *where* Grace had been hanging out all these years?

Specificity, specificity. My kingdom for a little specificity.

I went back to reading the message and almost choked on the last line. "As your powers continue to show up, go with the flow. - Aunt Fiona."

Wait.

"Go with the flow?" That's all you've got for me?

And "continue to show up?" There's *more* coming?

Didn't I have enough to deal with already?

So much for sleep. If I was going to be awake, I might as well be productive and start on my research.

I eased out of bed and went into the living room to retrieve the laptop. When I came back, Xavier had already appropriated the warm spot.

"Oh, no you don't," I scolded, picking him up and depositing him between Yule and Zeke. He didn't even bother to wake up.

I easily located the news reports about the discovery of skeletal remains on a hiking trail near Sparta. The skull showed signs of blunt force trauma consistent with the medical findings about Jane's death—and my fleeting perception of what may have been a tripod coming at my face.

Grace believed I stumbled and fell on the exact spot where Jane's body rested on the trail. Did that physical contact trigger my vision?

After several minutes with Google, I found a name for what happened to me—psychometry. Official definition: The supposed ability to discover facts about an event or person by touching inanimate objects associated with them.

I stared at the screen. The first time was an accident. Could I use the ability intentionally?

Glancing around the room, my eye fell on an antique music box sitting atop the high dresser in the corner. I remembered Aunt Fiona saying as she wound the box, "This is very precious to me, honey. I don't want anything to happen to it."

I got up again and walked over to the dresser. With great care, I picked up the antique and suddenly I was in a warm, cozy room with a huge Christmas tree in the corner by the fireplace. In my hands, I held a box wrapped in red and green paper. I could see my hands, or rather the hands of a child, carefully peeling the paper away.

Inside the package, the music box lay nestled in tissue. A little girl's awed voice said, "Oh, Papa, it's beautiful!" And then a man answered, "Open the lid, Fiona. It plays Chopin."

The first tinkling notes carried me back to my bedroom. Tears filled my eyes. The vision gave me a rare and wonderful gift—the sound of my grandfather's voice.

Almost reverently, I put the music box safely back in place. If I touched something that belonged to Grace, could I find her mother? But what could that "something" possibly be? So far, the only option was the poor girl's skeleton. I couldn't imagine waltzing into the coroner's office and saying, "Excuse me? Could I please touch those bones so I can get a vision and figure out who this poor kid really was?"

I would have made the request to help Grace, but the authorities would never agree.

Let me give you a word of advice disguised as literary foreshadowing. Most of the time when you think you have one option? Think again.

In the end, I let the cats have the bed. I curled up on the sofa and fell asleep. The next morning, I awakened to four furry miscreants sitting in a perfect row on the coffee table staring at me. No alarm clock needed in my household.

After they were fed, I had yogurt and toast, dressed, and went downstairs to greet the day. Or rather to greet Grace, who was, once again, standing at the front window watching people starting to come and go on Main Street.

"Good morning," I said.

"Hi," she answered. "Can you come here for a minute?"

"Sure," I said, walking over to join her. "What's going on?"

"Do you see that florist's shop over there by the library?" Grace asked.

"Yes. Why?"

"I think my homecoming corsage came from there."

I wanted to let out a celebratory whoop. This was our first sign of progress, but I contained myself. Too much pressure might destroy Grace's fragile memories.

"Are you sure?" I asked.

Grace nodded. "Pretty sure," she said. "And I think I have a library book that's overdue."

Uh oh. Unless the local library offered debt forgiveness, somebody was going to be in for a shock when that bill came due.

"Do you think you lived in Briar Hollow?" I asked cautiously.

"I think I was a cheerleader," Grace said suddenly. "For the Briar Hollow Bears."

Never mind name, age, and Social Security number. She knew the high school mascot.

"Let's go to the library," I said.

Grace's face fell. "I don't know where that book is," she said. "It was something for English class about catching grains."

Huh? Catching grains?

Oh. Wait.

Catcher in the Rye.

"Don't worry about the book," I said. "The librarian can't see you, and you wouldn't have liked the story anyway. Trust me."

The day was still young enough that I didn't have to be worried about customers. This errand couldn't wait. What if Grace's emerging memories started to fade?

She followed me across the square to the library housed in an old red brick building. The hinges of the front door squeaked alerting a stereotypical librarian, complete with gray bun. She stuck her head out of the room behind the counter.

"Good morning," she said. "Help yourself to coffee." She indicated a single-cup coffee maker and a carousel of assorted brew cups on a table under the front window that looked out on the square.

"Thank you," I said, "but I don't really have time to browse. I'm Jinx Hamilton. I inherited my Aunt Fiona's store across the square."

"Oh my goodness!" the woman exclaimed, coming out from behind the counter and engulfing me in a hug. "I'm Linda Albert. Fiona and I were in the same book club. I loved your aunt to pieces! She did pick some strange books for us to read sometimes, but my heavens, she was so much fun we didn't mind."

I wisely refrained from asking about Aunt Fiona's "strange" literary choices.

"It's nice to meet you, Linda. I was wondering if you could help me with something?"

"I'd love to, honey," she said. "What do you need?"

"Do you have old copies of the local high school yearbook?"

"You bet I do," she said. "All the way back to 1906. Come with me."

Grace and I followed Linda into a side room, where she

pointed out a long shelf filled with oversized volumes covered in various combinations of red and black, the local high school colors.

"Why in the world do you want to see old yearbooks?" Linda asked.

"Oh," I said, searching for a plausible excuse. "I'm just finding lots of things in the store that seem to be local heirlooms. Sports trophies and such. I thought I'd try to get them back to people who might care about them."

Linda seemed good with the thin fabrication. Before she could ask me anything else, the squeaking front-door hinges saved me.

"You come find me if you need anything else," Linda said, bustling toward the front. "Take all the time you want."

I turned to Grace and said in a low voice, "Are you ready to do this?"

She looked hopeful and terrified at the same time. "Yes," she said. "I want to know who I am."

Scanning the yearbooks, I pulled out the one for 1984, in case Grace's memory was off. It wasn't. We found her on the second page of the junior class portraits. Under the picture, the name read "Elizabeth 'Beth' Barlow." She had been a cheerleader, and judging from the list of other activities, a girl who did have fun.

Beside me, the ghost sighed. "I loved that blouse," she said simply.

"You remember?" I asked.

"Yes," she said. "But I don't know how I got up there in the woods."

The sound of voices from the other room made me rethink the wisdom of having this conversation where we might be overheard. Or rather where *I* might be overheard.

"Let's go back to the store," I suggested. "We can talk about it there."

Chapter Eighteen

On the way to the store a realization hit me. Not everyone lived and died by cell phone the way Tori and I did. The shop had a hardwired telephone, which meant there was probably a local phone book somewhere under the counter.

After a minute of rummaging, I produced a slender local directory printed on cheap paper and stuffed with advertisements. Thumbing to the *B* section, I ran my finger down the list: Barden, Barker, Barland, *Barlow*.

I looked up at the ghostly girl. "Does the name Emily Barlow mean anything to you?"

Beth nodded. "Yes, she's my mom. Can we go see her?"

It didn't seem to occur to Beth that she could go alone. Thirty years after her death, Beth couldn't shake her ingrained good manners. That, more than anything, confounded me about her death. How does a girl like that wind up getting murdered? I found it hard to believe Beth's story would turn out to be anything more than the classic "wrong place wrong time" storyline.

"I don't know your mom," I explained patiently. "I can't go over there and tell her that her daughter's ghost is with me and wants to talk. She'll think I'm nuts, or worse some kind of con artist trying to exploit her grief. Besides, we don't know what happened to you yet."

Beth pointed at my laptop sitting by the cash register. "Won't that tell us?" she asked. "My friend Joey had a Commodore 64, but I think your MacBook is smarter."

Uh, yeah. Steve Jobs did a grave spin on that one. But Beth had a point.

I opened the laptop, went to my browser, and searched Google for, "Beth Barlow Briar Hollow 1985."

Imagine reading the accounts of a missing girl's disappearance with the victim looking over your shoulder. In life, Beth was the most popular girl in the Briar Hollow High Class of 1985: she was head cheerleader, senior class favorite, an accomplished pianist, and president of the Future Homemakers of America.

Beth went missing on a Friday night after the homecoming game—still wearing the same corsage she'd remembered that morning. According to her grief-stricken mother, Beth asked for permission to attend a chaperoned, alcohol-free party after the game.

Witnesses at the party said Beth went to her car to get her jacket a little before eleven o'clock. It was midnight before her classmates realized she hadn't returned. Going to check on her, they found the car door open and her letter jacket lying on the front seat. There was no sign of a struggle. Beth was never seen again.

"Do you remember any of this?" I asked, turning toward the girl.

She nodded. "It was cold that night," she said. "The party was up at the Briar Hollow Family Campground in the big party room. When I went out to the car, someone came up behind me, I think. There was this rag over my nose, and it smelled awful. All gross and sweet."

I turned back to the computer and did another Google search. According to Wikipedia, chloroform is a "colorless, sweet-smelling, dense liquid."

"Somebody knocked you out," I said. "Do you remember anything after that?"

"I think I was in some kind of big, open space," she said. "Someone was taking pictures of me." Her form wavered in and out, a distortion signaling agitation and fear.

"I don't want to talk about that," she said, fading out again. "That's a bad thing, and I don't want to talk about it."

"That's okay," I said, quickly closing the laptop. "You don't have to talk about it. I promise."

My assurances seemed to help Beth to solidify herself, but her voice quivered when she said plaintively, "I want to go see the cats now."

"You go on, honey," I said. "They love it when you sit with them. Don't be upset, Beth. Everything will be okay."

I didn't even get the last words out before she was gone.

That evening when Tori called on Facetime, she frowned and leaned toward the camera. "What are you doing in the storeroom?" she asked. Then she spotted our resident rat sitting on my shoulder. "Hi, Rodney!"

I kid you not, Rodney picked up his paw and waved at the screen.

"He's going to talk one of these days," I said, looking at Rodney and then turning my attention back to Tori. "I'm downstairs because I really don't want Beth to hear all this again"

Tori frowned. "Who's Beth?"

"Grace," I answered. "Her real name is Elizabeth Barlow. She went missing after the homecoming game in 1985."

I explained everything I'd learned that day to Tori, who

listened without interrupting me until I got to the part about Beth's memory of the chloroform.

"Bastard," she muttered darkly.

"Agreed," I said. "Beth got so upset at that point that she didn't want to talk anymore, but she did say she thought she had been taken to a big, open place, and she remembered a camera."

"Let me correct myself," Tori said. "*Sick* bastard. So, you think the killer is someone local?"

"Maybe," I said, "but I am certain Beth is the only local *victim*. No other girls have gone missing in Briar Hollow since her disappearance."

I confirmed this fact after three hours of digging through the online files of the *Briar Hollow Banner*. Think "small town newspaper hell."

"Of course no other girls have gone missing in town," Tori said. "He couldn't take more locally. The risk of getting caught would be too high."

You see? You don't have to obsessively watch *CSI* and *Criminal Minds* to figure these things out.

"So why dump the bodies on the hiking trails?" I asked. "He could get caught doing that too."

The camera jiggled as Tori shifted on the sofa. Beside me, Rodney bobbed his head in time with the screen until her image stilled. "I've been thinking about that," she said. "He only dumped Jane. He buried Beth and the other girl."

"You looked her up?" I asked.

"Better than that," Tori said. "A couple of state troopers came in the cafe today. I told them I was one of the rule-breakers who found the skeleton up by Weber's Gap and asked if they thought there was a connection to the other body found near Sparta."

I could just see the innocent-eyed performance she'd put on

while no doubt keeping the troopers' coffee cups filled to the rim.

"What did they say?"

"Those bones were found pretty much the same way we said we found Grace," Tori explained. "A couple out bird watching crouched down by an old log to watch a bunch of turkeys. When the woman looked down, there was a skull by her foot."

I frowned. "Another skull beside a tree that had fallen over? That's no coincidence."

"I said that to the trooper," Tori told me. "He was the younger, better looking one, by the way."

Of course, he was.

"His partner was in the men's room," Tori went on. "He told me the official theory is that the killer buried the two girls at the base of those trees so he would have a marker. I think he planned to do the same thing with Jane's body, but something interrupted him, and he couldn't go back and finish the job."

"You mean the killer wanted a marker so he could visit where he left the bodies?" I asked. "God. That is disgusting."

"They say serial killers do that kind of thing all the time," she observed solemnly.

"Who are 'they?'"

"The people on the forums where I've been lurking," she answered. "These nut jobs are obsessed with sicko serial killers. Do you know that some of the women on the boards actually write letters to murderers in prison?"

I shuddered. "Thank God we can stop looking into this as soon as we find out Jane's name."

Tori looked at me like I had two heads. "We have to catch this guy," she said.

Note the once again dangerous usage of the word "we."

"No, *we* don't," I said sternly. "We promised a ghost we'd

figure out her name. Finding Beth was an accident. She wants to see her mother, and then she can move on."

"To where?" Tori asked seriously.

Okay. Unfair pop quiz.

"I don't know," I stammered. "Into that light people talk about."

Tori looked at me and then asked in her grown-up voice, "Jinx, have you even started trying to learn about your abilities?"

"Of course I have," I said defensively. "I told you about the psychometry."

Tori shook her head. "That was so you could understand what's happening to *you*. Have you started trying to understand what's happening to *them*? Powers like yours are meant to be used to help people. For starters, why are the girls still here?"

"Isn't it because they don't know who they are?" I said. "I mean, that's what the cemetery ghosts said."

"That's what they said because that's all they understand," Tori said. "Jinx, I know you've had a lot of surprises these last few days, but you have to get up to speed. From what I'm reading, these spirits may want justice. For all we know, there's another lonely ghost up on that trail in Sparta."

Oh no. No, no, no, no.

I didn't realize I was shaking my head until Tori started laughing.

"You already know what I'm going to say, don't you?" she asked.

"You're fixing to tell me we're going hiking next weekend, and I'm telling you we're not."

Tori knew me well enough to understand I was nearing my limit. "Okay," she said, "how about this? I'll send you a bunch of links and some book titles. You do the reading. If you don't come to the same conclusion, we won't go up to the other hiking trail. We'll make sure Beth sees her mother, and we'll try to figure out Jane's name and be done with it. Okay?"

I agreed, but I suspected there was a catch. Tori does not give up that easily. Color me right.

Chapter Nineteen

The rest of the week was normal—or as normal as life could be in a self-aware store with a hyper-intelligent rat and a resident teenage ghost.

If it sounds like I took all of this in stride, I'm telling the story the wrong way. Honestly, I think I always believed in the possibility of ghosts, but I never expected to have one living with me. For the most part, Beth seemed extraordinarily normal. We had conversations. She asked questions. She wanted to understand how the world had changed without her. I did my best to offer explanations and to feed her obvious interest.

But then, she would lapse into foggy confusion. She didn't always seem to comprehend that death is an incurable condition. This was particularly evident when she asked to see her mother. Those moments reminded me Beth was a child aching to go home. I had no idea how to facilitate a reunion or even if I should try.

For the heck of it, I watched a few episodes of *Ghost Whisperer* on Netflix. Come on! If Jennifer Love Hewitt couldn't always make people listen when she told them she saw dead folks, how was I supposed to do it?

The more I thought about the situation, the more troubled I became over how I was supposed to help Beth and Jane. Was it my job to get them to some sort of portal? This "door" everyone seems to talk about? Was I supposed to be the one to show them "the light"? If so, man, were we in trouble. In the celestial lighting department, I'm not even a 40-watt bulb.

And what was the deal with Aunt Fiona? She seemed to be rocking the afterlife. Was that because she was a witch, or because she died without any unfinished business weighing her down? Or was she really in the same situation as Beth and Jane and didn't want to tell me?

Tori and I talked every night about the wisdom of taking Beth to the cemetery to meet Jane. The longer we discussed it, the more we agreed that risky or not, the meeting needed to happen. We had to find out if any common ground existed between the two girls. Maybe Beth's improved memory would trigger an awakening.

For the time being, I settled on letting Beth do whatever gave her the most comfort. That amounted to sitting on my sofa watching TV with the cats. I did mention that Beth is a forever teenager, right?

All in all, she handled the culture shock well. Beth checked out in a *Dynasty* world and came back in the middle of *Keeping Up with the Kardashians*. Have you ever tried to explain to anyone that Kim is famous for being famous?

Everyday things I took for granted left Beth wide-eyed with wonder. My cell phone fascinated her. When she died, the average cell phone had a battery life of ten minutes and weighed five pounds.

I didn't mind answering her questions, and there were plenty of them. It made me feel like her big sister, but get your head wrapped around this idea. I was born *after* Beth died.

She had a lot of catching up to do, and I was her only source of information. It wasn't like she could use Google herself, although she certainly had me consulting the search engine daily.

I could easily have curled up on the sofa with them and pretended the topsy-turvy condition of my world didn't exist. I don't do well with disruption. I wanted a predictable life again.

I thrive on routine. Even with everything going on, I quickly settled into the rhythm of store life. The local soap maker came into town on Wednesday with a wonderful selection of her products. We struck up an agreement on the spot. She had a friend who raised alpacas to harvest the fiber, which she then spun and dyed by hand to make luscious scarves and sweaters. By Thursday, a small assortment of those items was also on display downstairs.

Myrtle appeared to approve of the changes. When I was alone in the store, I continued the process of rearranging and sorting. Sometimes, without my asking, that strange disembodied spotlight fell on a cabinet or drawer, and I'd find more merchandise in keeping with my current organizational scheme.

Every morning I went out and swept the front sidewalk, saying good morning first to Festus sunning on his bench, and then to Chase. My neighbor now watched for me daily and came out with a hot cup of coffee in each hand.

I enjoyed those few minutes at the start of the day and twice accepted his invitation to have a sandwich in his shop over the noon hour. We were still getting to know one another, so there were lively discussions about everything from books and cats, to my future plans for the store.

The contractor, Mark Haskell, dropped by and took measurements, promising to return Saturday morning when Tori was in town. He was enthusiastic about the project, and his early price estimates were beyond reasonable given the quality of the work I saw at the pizzeria.

All in all, life began to take on a satisfying sense of accomplishment. At some point each day, I took a few minutes to practice my ability to manipulate objects, improving my focus and control. I also tried a couple of cautious psychometry experiments.

According to my visions, the silver-headed cane in the umbrella stand belonged to a World War I veteran who carried a fragment of shrapnel from the Somme in his leg. The vintage, ladies' hat, complete with feather and net veil, harbored the details of a somewhat torrid affair between a local society matron and the Methodist minister from the 1950s.

Frankly, that kind of thing was fun, but serious metaphysical business also required my attention. Each day after I closed and locked the front door, I devoted the evening hours to research. That first morning when I levitated the figurine and had coffee with my dead aunt in the kitchen, "reality" became a multi-faceted concept for me.

If anyone had come to me with that story, by the way, "reality" is not the word I would have used. I probably would have asked what they had been smoking.

It's hard to describe my mindset during those first days, because my thoughts were all over the place. I like a healthy dose of good fortune as well as the next person. Give me a rabbit's foot; I'll carry it. But frankly, I think you'll cultivate better karma leaving it on the rabbit where it belongs.

Over the years, I've certainly thrown my fair share of coins into wishing wells. I don't risk walking under ladders. Friday the 13th is not my favorite day in any month. In the magic/superstition category I'd say I'm average—or at least I was until life threw me a curveball.

Aunt Fiona's wine bottle note said my powers were still

sorting themselves out. That added an element of uncertainty to daily life that challenged my coping skills. I needed to take charge.

Tori made a good suggestion when she told me to study what it really means to be a witch dealing with ghosts and God only knows what else.

Judging from the extensive list of web links and books Tori emailed to me, she was several steps ahead of me in the "learning how to be a witch's best friend" category.

I wasn't silly enough to think that a wart would suddenly appear on the end of my nose or that I needed to run out and buy a pointy black hat. I did wonder, however, if I needed to join a coven or try to meet others like myself. Was there a union? Or, for that matter, *were* there any others like me?

Aunt Fiona said she gifted me with my magical powers. Did that rule out the possibility that being a witch was hereditary? Suddenly, I was filled with questions and hungry for answers.

In my childhood, my mother dragged me to church enough that I was now vaguely uneasy that I might be involved in something associated with devil worship. Getting my head wrapped around the notion of "white" witches versus "black" witches took up the better part of a day.

After reading several Wiccan websites, I was relieved to learn that the religion doesn't divide the world into opposing camps of ultimate good and ultimate evil. Satan is a Christian construct. I was good with him getting the heck behind me and staying there. All the Wiccan pages talked about being in balance with nature, which I immediately liked. I mean seriously, isn't that the basis for the Golden Rule?

But then I came to understand that modern Wicca occupies the tip of the witch iceberg. There are many, many traditions of witchcraft spread out over centuries of folklore and mythology from all over the world. Something Joseph Campbell talked about in *The Power of Myth* blew my mind. A myth isn't necessarily false; it's somebody else's explanation for what you call religion.

For the first time in my life, I wasn't thinking outside the proverbial box—I was building a different box altogether.

Please don't get the idea that I simply took a few days and figured everything out. It's an ongoing process. Asking questions and learning new things is what my life is about now. Actually, I think it's a major part of *being* alive. If my new identity as a witch has brought me anything, it's a reawakening of my native curiosity and a reopening of my heart to the potential for miracles.

That's happy stuff, people. In fact, it's often downright joyous.

There's more in the world we don't understand than what we do. From my perspective, that's pretty darn cool.

That realization changed my thinking about going after the third ghost. With potential opening up before me, how could I deny that same magic to girls whose spirits were trapped in an existence not of their choosing?

I didn't understand why Jane and Beth were different from Aunt Fiona or Colonel Longworth. All I knew about ghostly social structure came from my initial conversation with the Colonel.

He told me Aunt Fiona believed unfinished business trapped the spirits within the graveyard walls. That explanation held up fine until Beth appeared. Her grave wasn't in a cemetery and she had complete freedom of movement. Not knowing the identity of your murderer qualified as "unfinished business," but Jane cared more about discovering her name than learning who killed her.

Yeah, yeah, I know. Every rule has an exception, which does nothing to make the exceptions less annoying.

There was one thing I did know. Jane and Beth weren't happy, or even content like the other cemetery ghosts. I might not be able to help any of these spirits find a light to walk into, but I *might* be able to give the murdered girls a measure of peace.

When Tori arrived at the shop around five o'clock Friday afternoon, Myrtle played the *Ghostbusters* theme.

"Way to steal a girl's thunder, Myrtle," I said, as the music died down.

As Tori hugged me hello, she asked, "Does that mean what I think it means?"

"Yeah," I said, hugging her back. "We're going looking for another ghost."

Chapter Twenty

We had a big Saturday. Mark Haskell dropped by around 9:30 with Chase in tow. My next-door neighbor and potential boyfriend was a man of many interests. He explained that he enjoyed doing carpentry work and sometimes helped Mark out on his jobs.

Since this project would be right next door, it made perfect sense for him to lend a hand, didn't it?

The whole thing sounded like an excuse for Chase to spend more time in my near vicinity, which left me floating on cloud nine.

Tori and Mark hit it off immediately. His initial designs dovetailed neatly with her ideas. They worked together for about an hour to refine the overall concept, while Chase and I offered suggestions from the sidelines. Chase seemed to have a good sense of space, and I was intrigued by some of his creative solutions for storage options.

After Mark left, Chase asked if Tori and I would join him for supper that night. I was genuinely disappointed to have to tell him we had another obligation. He accepted the news with graceful flexibility and suggested instead that we all have Sunday dinner at the pizzeria so Tori could meet Pete.

That option suited all concerned perfectly. We made firm plans to convene out in front of the store at eleven o'clock the next morning in order to beat the church crowd. Chase said he'd give Pete the heads up so Tori would be able to see his living space.

As Tori watched Chase exit the store, she said, "Oh. My. God. Jinx. He's an absolute dream."

Feigning innocence I said, "Which one? Mark or Chase?"

She gave me a mock punch in the arm. "Chase. Mark was wearing a wedding ring."

I sighed happily. "Yeah," I agreed. "He's pretty dreamy, but so is Pete. I'm glad you're going to have a chance to meet him tomorrow."

"I could do with some dreamy," Tori said ruefully. "It would be a nice change of pace from 'nightmare.'"

There was nothing I would like better than to see Tori dating a nice man who truly appreciated her. We were both due to draw good numbers in the romance lottery.

With our social life in order and the renovation jump-started, Tori and I prepared to drive to the hiking trail where the third girl was found. If we located the victim's spirit, we had a plan. We would ask her to return to Briar Hollow with us for a ghostly summit conference that evening at the cemetery.

I refused to ask Beth to go to the graveyard without explaining the potential consequences to her. The night before, Tori and I described the invisible barrier that kept the spirits confined and asked Beth how she felt about coming with us to meet Jane.

I wasn't surprised when the girl resisted. "If I get trapped in there," she said in a worried voice, "then I can't be with the cats."

Nothing gave Beth a greater sense of stability than my four

furry hooligans. I quietly blessed them for being so attentive to her and rewarded them with extra helpings from the small, expensive cans of chow they favored. Though welcome, the bribe wasn't necessary. The cats seem to understand that Beth truly needed them, and they responded to her with loving devotion.

Ultimately Beth agreed to a compromise. She would come with us but stay outside the cemetery fence. Tori could see Beth consistently now, even when I was not present, so she would stand at the gate and relay anything Beth said to me.

I would be inside the graveyard talking to Jane. The arrangement would be cumbersome, an otherworldly version of translating a United Nations' session, but Beth wouldn't agree to anything else.

As Tori and I prepared to leave on Saturday, she asked me, yet again, "Should we tell Beth where we're going?"

We'd gone back and forth on the issue of full disclosure for good reason.

"I still think the idea of asking another ghost to the party will freak her out," I said. "Talking about introducing her to Jane upset her enough already. If we do get the other girl to come home with us, we'll have to wing it when we tell Beth."

Initially, we intended to share the whole plan with Beth but abandoned the idea the evening before when the girl began fading in and out during our conversation.

"I don't blame her for getting stressed out," Tori said. "A few more spirits and this place will turn into a ghostly sorority house."

How's that for a terrifying image?

"Yeah," I said. "I don't want to see that happen. The idea isn't to adopt the ghosts, it's to get them to move on."

Do I even need to point out that being the crazy ghost lady is way worse than being the crazy cat lady?

With an hour's drive ahead followed by a 45-minute hike,

we packed a picnic lunch. Spring gifted us with another gorgeous day. We both enjoyed the trip, talking non-stop the whole way.

Tori filled me in about the new waitresses currently on probation at Tom's but changed the subject when I asked if she'd talked to her mom about the impending move.

"You can't put it off forever," I warned.

Giving her studious attention to the passing landscape, Tori said, "Oh, look. Trees."

"Nice try, kiddo. Seriously, how mad can Gemma be?"

"I don't know," Tori said. "How mad was your mom?"

She had me there. We let the subject drop.

The map application on Tori's phone led us directly to the trailhead. Without the help we might have missed the sign entirely.

"People have to know about this place to find it," I said as I climbed out of the Prius and pulled my daypack out of the backseat.

"Maybe that's why the killer thought it would be a good place to dump a body," Tori said, shouldering her own pack.

The ghoulish tone of our conversation seemed odd in a place filled with such natural beauty and peaceful stillness. As I locked the car, a squirrel chattered a greeting to us from high up in a tree and nearby a woodpecker hammered out an industrious rhythm.

Sounds. Not noise. Hence "stillness."

Even though we were there to locate the ghost of a murdered girl, I felt tension I didn't know I carried drain from my system.

As we started up the gentle incline into the mountains, no one would have thought we were anything other than a couple of hikers out to enjoy the day.

This excursion proved more difficult than the one we'd taken to Weber's Gap. No memorial stone marked the place where the remains of the girl were discovered. We now referred to her as "Twenty-Five."

I know. Calling her a number seemed cold to us, too, but ghost naming was getting complicated. "Twenty-Five" worked because her disappearance fit the pattern chronologically between Beth and Jane.

A downtrodden strip of grass leading off to one side of the trail marked our destination. The temporary path led to a dug-up area at the base of a massive hickory tree. Telltale pieces of yellow crime scene tape still draped the underbrush.

"This looks like the place," I said. "Now what?"

"I guess you do your thing," Tori said, making a little "go on" motion with her hand.

My *thing*? Oh, yeah. That helped.

"Oh, really," I said in exasperation. "My thing? What is that exactly?"

"Whatever you did with the other two?" Tori offered weakly.

"The other two came to me. I have no idea how to summon a ghost."

"Why don't you try asking?" an angry, sarcastic voice said from behind me. "Or is that too polite for you high-and-mighty living people?"

I almost jumped out of my skin.

Why the heck do they always have to do that?

When I whirled around, Tori got the message that we were no longer alone. "Do we have incoming?" she asked.

"We have contact," I answered.

Tori looked over my left shoulder and gasped. We found the third ghost, alright, but she was nothing like Jane and Beth.

The other girls looked much as I imagined they had in life. This spirit bore the marks of the cruel abuses that took her life. She'd been hit in the head with such force the entire left side of her skull sagged inward. A frozen river of dried blood ran down her neck and into her filthy, torn blouse. I didn't have to be a doctor to know no one could have survived a blow like that.

She glared at us with red-rimmed eyes and demanded sharply, "What the hell are you looking at?"

Not exactly the reception we had in mind.

"Uh, hi," I said lamely. "I'm Jinx and this is Tori."

"What did you do with my body?" the girl said furiously. "I want it back. Now."

"We didn't have anything to do with your body being taken away," I said. "We came up here to try to help you."

"Help me by giving me my body back!" the girl screamed.

Even though the sun was still shining brightly, the air around us turned cold and clammy. I felt a prickly, electric sensation pulsing up my arms. The girl took a menacing step toward us. Instinctively, I put my hand up. When I did, an arc of blue light shot out from my fingertips and spread into a shield-like field that held the spirit at bay.

"Whoa!" Tori said. "Good one."

The ghost was no longer coming toward us, but sheer fury rolled off her in palpable waves. "I want my body back," she said again. "You had no right to take it away."

Okay. Let's try this again.

"The police took your body away," I said. "We aren't the police, and we don't want to hurt you."

"You can't hurt me," the girl said. "I've already been hurt." As she spoke, she raised her hand and pushed her long, tangled hair aside to reveal the true devastation to her ruined head. "Hurt" was an understatement.

"Who did that to you?" I asked.

"He did it," the ghost said. "He told me I was beautiful, and then he turned me into this."

"Who was 'he?'" I pressed. "We think he hurt others like you. We want him to be punished."

The ghost threw her head back and screamed again. "I don't care about the others! He took everything from *me*. Doesn't anybody care about *me*?"

"Narcissistic much?" Tori muttered.

"We care about you," I said, lowering my hand. As I did, the blue light dimmed, and the shield grew smaller. "See? I don't want to hurt you. If I make the light go away completely will you talk to us?"

I tried to sound like I knew what I was doing, which I didn't —at all.

"What do you want?" The words came out in a snarl, but the spirit didn't try to charge us again.

"I want to know anything you remember about the person who did this to you," I said.

"He asked me why I couldn't be good and do as I was told like the first one."

"Do you know who the first one was?"

"Little Miss Rah Rah," she sneered. "He showed me the pictures."

Beth. She was a cheerleader, and she remembered a camera.

"Do you know your own name?" I asked. "Can you tell us who you are?

A look of painful confusion washed over her features. "I was *someone*," she said, her voice rising again. "He took me because he thought I was nobody. But I was *somebody*. I was!"

The wind howled as she surged forward. I brought my hand up. The ghost collided with the blue light igniting a blinding flash, and then we were alone again.

"Holy unhappy haunting, Batman," Tori said. "That is one seriously pissed off ghost."

Chapter Twenty-One

So much for the theory all ghosts enjoy a fairly benign afterlife and the idea I can't work magic outside of the shop. Tori and I came about halfway back down the trail before we stopped to eat lunch to put distance between us and the less-than-blithe spirit.

"At least we know we have the order of the killings right," Tori said, unwrapping her turkey sandwich. "First Beth, then Anger Management Girl, and then Jane."

"Those are the killings we know of," I pointed out as I opened a bag of chips. "There could have been others."

"You know what I think?" Tori asked, taking two chips and munching contemplatively.

"What?"

"I think Twenty-Five was a runaway. That could be why she said she was taken, because the killer thought she was a nobody. She might not have even been from this part of the country."

That would explain a lot. Even street-smart runaways could get desperate for help and fall in with the wrong person.

"Maybe Jane was a runaway, too," I suggested. "Which

kind of makes it pointless to take Beth to the cemetery tonight."

"No," Tori said, "it doesn't."

"Why not?"

"They both saw the killer," she said. "All we need is for one of them to remember something."

"You know," I answered uneasily, "I realize we've already talked this to death, but I'm still not so sure about that part. I mean, I know we want to solve the murders and help them move on, whatever that means, but is it right to ask the girls to relive what happened to them?"

Tori considered that. "Are you thinking they went through something like what happened to Twenty-Five?"

"According to the authorities, both Beth and Jane died of blunt force trauma to the head," I said. "They must have been hurt the same way. We only saw Beth's skull from the front. We have no idea what the damage to her head really looked like."

"True," Tori conceded. "But if she and Jane were killed like that, why do they look normal now? I mean 'normal' as in dead, but not gross dead like Twenty-Five."

I shook my head. "I don't know, maybe because they were happier people in real life? Regardless, I'm not sure it's right for us to ask them to re-experience the last horrible minutes of their lives."

"They do seem fragile," Tori admitted. "According to the other ghosts at the cemetery, Jane is sad all the time, and she cries a lot. Beth winks on and off like Christmas lights."

"She does that when she's nervous," I said defensively.

I sounded like an overprotective parent making excuses for her child.

"I know," Tori said placatingly. "I wasn't criticizing Beth. She kind of grows on you, doesn't she?"

"Yes, she does," I said. "I mean, would it really be so bad for her to stay with us at the store?"

There it was. I finally said it. I wanted to adopt a ghost.

"No," Tori said contemplatively, "it wouldn't be so bad. All she wants to do is sit on the sofa with the cats and watch TV. It's not like she's a problem for anybody, but don't you think the choice has to be up to her? Isn't it up to us to give her options?"

That was a point I hadn't considered at all.

Beth wasn't making any choices on her own. She went along with whatever we said. I was the one who thought of death as an incurable condition, and yet the ghosts at the cemetery seemed to accept their existence, confined or not. Aunt Fiona enjoyed death so much she would probably be on the cover of the next afterlife edition of *People*.

Who did I think I was talking about sending Beth and Jane anywhere? Our goal should be to empower the girls. They weren't stray cats who needed a home or, worse yet, projects to be completed.

Tori wanted to do for them what she routinely does for me: present options for exploration.

"You know," I said, looking at Tori fondly, "sometimes you're pretty smart."

She gave me a look of doe-eyed innocence. "Who, me?"

"Okay," I said, "the cemetery it is."

I started to bag up the remains of my lunch. The first rule of being a good steward of nature? Leave nothing but footprints.

Before I could finish, Tori put her hand on my arm. I looked up questioningly.

"Uh, Jinksy," she said. "We're kind of not done with this conversation. What the heck did you do up there anyway?"

Oh. That blue light cosmic ghost-repelling shield thing? Yeah, I guess that was conversation worthy.

"I honestly don't know," I admitted. "I think I reversed the power I use to bring things toward me. I really believed I could only use magic like that inside the store with Myrtle's help."

"Were you trying to stop Twenty-Five?"

"Not really," I said. "It just happened. I was afraid she was going to hurt us. I wanted to push her away. Putting my hand up was a reflex. The next thing I know, I'm all Miss Laser Light Show."

"It was impressive," Tori said. "The automatic reverse thing makes sense."

"Huh?"

"Well, if you can pull something, you ought to be able to push it, too. Isn't a law of motion we learned in science class junior year? Something the apple guy said?"

She meant Sir Isaac Newton, not Steve Jobs.

For every action, there is an equal and opposite reaction.

Loose translation, if I can pull, I can also push. Did that mean all my powers had a reverse mode?

That was too much for me to think about at the moment and I said so. "TMI, Tori," I declared. "Let's be glad the Push-Me / Pull-Me thing worked and that Twenty-Five left us alone."

"Trust me," Tori said shuddering, "this is me being glad, very glad."

We walked back to the car in silence, letting the peaceful landscape take the edge off our ghostly encounter. I believed we could help Beth and Jane, but I wasn't sure about this latest ghost. What level of justice could possibly make up for what she experienced?

File that question away for future reference. We're not done with it.

On the way home, I spotted a sign for the Briar Hollow Family Campground. "Hey! That's where Beth was the night she disappeared," I said. "Let's have a look around."

Pulling off the back-country road, I guided the Prius down

a dirt lane for about a mile and a half. The campground was exactly what I would have expected. A temporary community of recreational vehicles and tents sat grouped around a massive building constructed to resemble a vintage barn.

"That must be where the party was held," I said.

Just then, an older man wearing a beat up, disheveled hat waved us to a stop.

When I rolled the window down, he barked, “Campers only. No Lookie Loos. Turn around and get out.”

“I am so sorry, sir,” I said, putting on my best manners. “I’m new in town and my friend and I were exploring the countryside. We didn’t mean to break the rules.”

He regarded me with keenly suspicious eyes. “New in town?” he rasped. “Doing what?”

“My aunt, Fiona Ryan, ran a store on the courthouse square,” I said. “She left it to me.”

To my utter astonishment, the old coot threw his head back and let out a cackling rattle of laughter. “Fiona Ryan’s niece. Now that’s rich.”

“Excuse me?” I said, a hint of ice creeping into my tone.

“There was no love lost between me and that crazy aunt of yours,” he snapped. “Now get the hell off my land and don’t come back.”

“Not a problem,” I said, rolling the window up and putting the car in reverse. I spun the tires, which is not easy to do in a Prius. Our exit called for a display of attitude.

“What the heck was his problem?” Tori asked, peering in the rearview mirror.

“I have no idea,” I said. “But if Aunt Fiona didn’t like him, neither do I.”

Maybe not the most mature statement I made that day, but true all the same.

Chapter Twenty-Two

Right up to the moment she floated out of the door behind us that night, Beth came up with excuses why she shouldn't accompany us to the graveyard.

On the stairs, I stopped and turned toward her. "You really don't have to come," I said, making sure the words sounded as kind as I intended them to be. "I know this idea frightens you."

An odd thing happened. Beth's form grew brighter and more substantial. The girl cocked her head to one side and asked slowly, "What did you say?"

I repeated, "I know this frightens you."

"You do?" she said, note of wonder in the words. "And you're not mad at me?"

Where the heck did that come from?

"Of course I'm not mad at you," I said. "Everybody gets scared sometimes."

"Okay," she said. "I'll come."

Tori looked at me with raised eyebrows. I shrugged. What did I know about teenagers and their moods?

I parked the car off to one side of the graveyard where it

couldn't be seen from the road. As the three of us approached the iron gate I said, "Beth, you wait here."

She nodded, her eyes wide and luminous. I opened the gate and stepped inside, only to be instantly greeted by the ghost of Colonel Beau Longworth.

"Good evening, Miss Jinx," he said, sweeping off his hat and offering me a courtly bow.

"Hi, Beau," I said. "How are you?"

"Dear lady," he said, smiling rakishly, "in my present state, I fear I am always the same. Quite dead."

Well, at least he had a positive attitude about the condition.

Tori, who stood with one foot outside the cemetery and the other inside, said, "Hi, Beau."

Longworth turned toward her. "Why are you standing there, Miss Tori? Please, come in."

"I need her to be where she is, Beau," I said, launching into an explanation of why we'd come to the graveyard that night.

The old soldier listened patiently, shaking his head sadly as I told him about Beth. "I fear this town harbors a cowardly, black-hearted killer," he said.

"I think so, too," I agreed. "Beth is afraid she will become trapped here like the rest of you."

"A wise apprehension on the part of the young lady," he said. "We do, however, have something of a problem. Miss Jane rarely leaves the vicinity of her grave. I'm not sure if she will join us for this conversation."

That I hadn't counted on.

"Will you come with me to talk to her?"

"It would be my honor," he said.

I started to tell Tori we'd be back as soon as we could, but the young football player had her cornered. He was eagerly asking about the latest sports news. Tori obligingly called up the headlines on her phone and started reading a story to him about the NFL draft. She glanced up, saw me looking at her, and nodded her understanding about where I was going.

As Colonel Longworth and I strolled toward Jane's grave, I smiled at the two ladies in gingham we'd seen on our last visit. They raised their hands in greeting before going on with their conversation.

"Things seem quiet tonight," I observed.

"The moon is in its waning phase," Beau said. "We are at our best under its full rays."

That was an interesting tidbit of information to file away.

"You seem like your usual self," I said.

"As I told you before, Miss Jinx, I am old," the Colonel admitted. "One gets good at anything with sufficient practice, even death."

We found Jane sitting forlornly on the ground beside her simple headstone. I squatted down so I would be at eye level with her. "Hi, Jane," I said. "Remember me?"

"Yes," she said in a low tone. "Have you found out who I am?"

"Not yet, honey," I said. "But I've brought someone with me who might be able to help. She's like you."

Jane studied me for a moment. "You mean she's dead?"

I nodded.

"And somebody did something bad to her?"

"Yes," I said. "Somebody hurt her the same way you were hurt."

"Was it the same somebody?" she asked fearfully. "He's not here, too, is he?"

"No, he's not here," I assured her. "I do think the same person hurt you both. I was hoping you might try to talk to her so we can figure that out for sure. Her name is Beth."

"That's a pretty name."

"She's waiting by the front gate," I said.

"I don't go up there," Jane said. "She has to come here."

Beside me, Beau cleared his throat. "Miss Jane?"

The girl looked up and the Colonel went on. "My dear child, you do understand that none of us can leave this place, do you not?"

Jane nodded.

"Miss Beth fears to enter the cemetery lest she become trapped with us," Beau said. "You must speak to her through the gate."

"I can't go up there," she said, her voice breaking. "If he sees me, he'll hurt me again."

Colonel Longworth's mouth set in a firm line. "No one will hurt you, Jane. You have my word of honor that I will protect you at every moment."

Jane regarded him solemnly. "When you were alive, did you have a little girl?" she asked.

The question took Longworth unawares. He looked uncertain for a moment, then said gruffly, "I left behind a wife and a daughter. My sons were killed at the Battle of Gettysburg."

"I bet you were a good father," Jane said, getting up and holding out her hand. "I'll go with you."

Longworth took her hand and tucked it into the crook of his arm. I had to look away and swallow hard to keep from crying as they started to walk away.

"Are you coming, Miss Jinx?" the Colonel called over his shoulder.

"Right behind you," I answered.

As Jane and Longworth approached the cemetery gate, the other spirits gathered in curious knots. Obviously, the Colonel hadn't exaggerated when he said Jane never strayed far from her grave.

Beau quietly and carefully explained to Jane how the conversation with Beth would take place through Tori. Jane nodded that we should go ahead, so I told her everything we knew about Beth and the night she was abducted.

The girl frowned when I mentioned the campground.

"Camping?" she said. "You mean like when people use sleeping bags?"

"Yes," I said. "Have you ever been camping?"

"Maybe," she said. "Is there a barn there?"

"There is," I said, "but not a barn for livestock. It's where people have parties and meetings."

"You have to clean up after a party," Jane said flatly.

This could be a long night.

"Somebody has to clean up," I agreed.

"You don't get paid much money for that," Jane said. "But the food was good."

Suddenly, her disjointed statements began to hang together more coherently.

"Tori," I said, "ask Beth what kind of food they had at the party."

Oddly enough, from inside the cemetery, I couldn't hear Beth speak.

Tori listened for a minute and then said, "She said it was a barbecue. There's was a big pit . . ."

"In the barn," Jane finished. "The smoke smelled good. Not like the rag."

A warning bell went off in my head.

"What did the rag smell like?" I asked.

"Awful," Jane said, gagging. "Sweet."

Chloroform.

From the gate, Tori said, "Beth wants to know if Jane remembers the camera."

Jane's eyes went wide. "Click click," she said, "click click click click."

We'll go with a "yes" on the camera.

Tori listened, a sick look coming over her face. "Beth wants to know if Jane was a good girl and did what the man said."

At that, Jane started backing away making frightened, incoherent sounds. Colonel Longworth tried to soothe her. "It's alright, my dear," he said gently. "No one will hurt you in this place."

She looked up at him with pleading eyes. "I was a bad girl," she said. "Bad girl. Bad girl." With that, she turned and fled back to her grave.

Longworth looked at the women in gingham. "Ladies," he said, "would you see to her, please?"

The women glided away making anxious, clucking noises. Longworth turned to me. "I fear we will not get her to talk further this evening."

"She doesn't need to," I said. "We've heard all we need to know. I'm so sorry we frightened her, Beau."

"You had no intention to do harm," he said. "If you will pardon me, I want to check on her now."

As I watched the old soldier hurry away, I had to agree with Jane. I'd bet any amount of money Beau Longworth was a good father.

I found Tori outside the gate attempting to calm Beth who was gliding back and forth along the wall wringing her hands in intense agitation. Her form was fluctuating so badly, she almost disappeared entirely at one point.

"Mama always said do as I was told," the girl cried. "She said if I did as I was told everything would be alright. So I did as I was told, and it wasn't alright. It just wasn't."

"Has she said anything else?" I asked Tori in a whisper.

"No," Tori said. "Only that she's afraid we're going to punish her."

Dear God. That wasn't even a remote possibility.

"Beth, honey, calm down," I said, approaching her slowly.

The girl looked at me with wide, earnest eyes. "I was good," she said. "I was. I'm not lying. I was good."

"You *are* good," I said. "You really helped us tonight. Thank you."

Beth faltered. "I helped?" she asked in a small voice.

"Yes," I said. "You did. Are you ready to go home now and see that cats?"

"You're not mad at me?" she asked. Her form still flickered nervously, but she seemed stronger.

"No," I said. "I'm very, *very* proud of you."

With some cajoling, Beth got into the car with us for the short home. Myrtle made a concerned sound when we walked in the door.

"It's okay, Myrtle," I said. "Beth got a little scared at the cemetery."

The store answered me with a disapproving rumble.

"I know," I said. "I'm sorry. I shouldn't have let that happen."

Turning to Beth, I said, "Why don't you go see the cats? Tori and I will be up in a little bit."

The girl needed no encouragement. She was gone almost before I finished speaking.

Chapter Twenty-Three

Tori and I went into the storeroom expecting to sit at the table and talk, only to find the table gone. The room now sported a beat-up old easy chair, a sagging loveseat, and a wood box doing double duty as a coffee table.

"Where did all this come from?" Tori said.

Before I could tell her that I had no idea, Myrtle let out with a quiet trumpet fanfare over our heads.

Myrtle could materialize furniture?

Never mind. I didn't want to know.

As soon as I plopped down in the chair, which fit my body like a glove, Rodney scampered along the edge of the shelf and jumped onto my shoulder.

"Did you have anything to do with this?" I asked the rat.

Rodney gave the rodent version of a shrug and wiggled his whiskers as if to say, "You like?"

"I like," I said.

"Me, too," Tori agreed, making herself at home on the loveseat. "We needed a place to hang out when we're downstairs. We can call it the Rat Cave."

Rodney stood up on his hind legs and performed a maneuver that looked exactly like a fist pump.

"See," Tori said. "Rodney approves."

He approved even more when I broke into the cracker stash. While Tori and I talked, I could hear the rat munching away beside my right ear. When I stole a glance to see how much of a mess he was making on my blouse, I discovered him picking up his crumbs. As I watched, he reached down and brushed off the fabric.

From the loveseat, Tori said, "That was an intense graveyard summit."

"And then some," I said. "I hope Beau and the ladies were able to calm Jane down."

We agreed that, based on what we heard that night, the killer appeared to be trying to get his other victims to mimic behavior he found satisfying in Beth. The sick creep found compliant victims satisfying. Neither Jane nor Twenty-Five performed to his specifications. In Twenty-Five's case, severe violence ensued. But why the five-year lull between kills?

Neither one of us expected to solve anything that night. We wanted to give Beth time alone with the cats to recover. Finally, I could not keep my eyes open any longer. We went upstairs to find Beth happily covered in felines and restored to her usual placid self.

"I'm sorry, Beth," I said, "but we're both exhausted, and Tori sleeps on the sofa when she's here."

"Oh, that's not a problem," Beth said. "I'll go downstairs. Thank you for taking me with you tonight."

Dang. Whoever drilled manners into this girl did do one heck of a job.

"Uh, you're welcome," I said awkwardly.

You're welcome for a lovely night of trauma recalling your murder in terrifying detail, I added mentally.

Tori and I took turns in the bathroom, and then it was

lights out. About ten minutes later, she said, in a groggy voice, "Jinksy? You still awake?"

"Barely," I mumbled. "What?"

"Do you think I should wear my green blouse to meet Pete or the red one with the stripes?"

That's my gal. Always keeping her priorities straight.

The next morning, Tori insisted on trying on both blouses twice before settling on the green. I went wardrobe angst as well, but I kept it to myself.

Okay. Maybe I did change outfits.

Once.

Regardless, we still met Chase out in front of the store promptly at eleven.

"Hi!" he said cheerfully. "You both look great today."

Mission accomplished.

We thanked him as we stepped off the curb to commit blatant jaywalking. Trust me. Briar Hollow does not have a rush hour, especially with the whole town in church.

Pete, who I now discovered did have a last name—Miller—greeted us at the door of the pizzeria. Since we were his first customers, he gave us a quick apartment tour for Tori's benefit. She took pictures of some of the hardware and other details she liked, and then we claimed a prime table by the window before heading for the buffet.

While we filled our plates, Pete deposited a pitcher of sweet tea and three generous-sized glasses on our table. We came back loaded down with crisp salads and sinful pizza slices, diving into our food with enthusiasm.

By ten minutes of noon, other customers started to filter in including Sheriff John Johnson. Spying me and Tori, he waved and made his way over to speak.

"Good morning, Miss Hamilton, Miss Andrews," he said, nodding to each of us before adding, "Hey, Chase."

"Hey yourself, John," Chase said. "Care to join us?"

"Just for a minute," he said. "I wanted to tell Miss Hamilton and her friend what we've learned about that skeleton they found."

"It's Jinx and Tori," I corrected him. "Have the remains been identified?"

"They have," he said sadly. "She was a local girl, Elizabeth Barlow. Went missing back in 1985 after the homecoming game."

"Oh," Tori said, playing her part beautifully. "That's awful! Was she . . . I mean did someone . . ."

Her words trailed off, delicately avoiding descriptives like "kill" and "murder," which caused Sheriff Johnson to assume an even more protectively official air than he already displayed.

"I'm afraid it was a case of foul play, yes," he said gravely. "She was killed by a blow to the cranium."

Chase shook his head. "How is Emily taking the news?"

What? Chase knew Beth's mom? My turn to act innocent.

"Who is Emily?" I asked.

"Beth's mother," Chase explained. "She was in a car accident when she was a girl. Her left leg is shorter than her right. She brings her shoes to me, and I build the sole up so she can walk more easily. How is she, John?"

The Sheriff scrubbed at his face and let out a tired sigh. "Even after thirty years, she wasn't ready to hear that we'd found her daughter like that. But I think part of her is glad to have the closure. We're going to release the body as soon as possible. She wants to have a funeral."

"Do you have any idea who killed Elizabeth?" Tori asked.

"Beth," Sheriff Johnson said. "Everyone called her Beth. There was a suspect at the time, but no concrete evidence. He's an irascible old bas. . . er. . . reprobate now. I don't think he killed her, but I do believe he knew more than he was willing to say."

"This person was someone Beth knew?" I said.

"In passing," the Sheriff replied. "He runs the campground where she was abducted. The kids were having a party up there after the big game. Fellow named Woodrow Evers."

Tori and I exchanged a covert glance.

"Oh my," I said. "I think we met him yesterday by accident. Did this all happen at the Briar Hollow Family Campground?"

"It did," Johnson said, arching his eyebrows. "What were the two of you doing up there?"

"We drove to Sparta to meet our mothers and go shopping," I lied smoothly. "On the way home, I saw the sign for the campground and turned in out of curiosity. Mr. Evers ordered us off the property and was really nasty when I told him Fiona was my aunt."

"You're lucky he didn't take a shot at you," Johnson laughed. "He's been known to do that. Winged a bullet past an electrical company crew a couple of years ago when they planned to re-route some lines across his place. They were threatening to cut down one of his trees. Danged if he didn't take the whole thing to court and win. All that nonsense over a hickory tree when the woods are full of them."

A hickory tree? Like the ones Beth and Twenty-Five were buried under?

"Did he have a sentimental attachment to the tree?" I asked.

"Who knows," Johnson said. "The guy is an eccentric nut. Claimed the tree was a 'cultural treasure' due to its age, got a bunch of environmentalists on his side. They paid for his defense. Pretty slick deal."

"Why didn't he like Aunt Fiona?" I asked.

"Trust me," Sheriff Johnson said, "the bad feeling was mutual. Fiona opposed saving that damned hickory tree."

My back-to-nature, hippy, peace-loving, crazy witch aunt

was in *favor* of somebody cutting down a tree? There had to be more to *that* story.

"Anyway," the Sheriff said, standing up, "I promised I'd let you know. Wish I could tell you we had the killer, but on a 30-year-old case, that's not likely to happen. At least you've given Emily something to bury. Thank you for that."

As we watched him head for the buffet line, Tori said, "We should go to the service to pay our respects, since we're the ones who found her."

I knew what that meant.

We should go so we could take Beth with us.

So *not* on my bucket list.

Chapter Twenty-Four

Since we couldn't speak freely about Beth in front of Chase, the remainder conversation stayed blessedly murder free. Chase knew nothing about the events of the last week and didn't realize the more ectoplasmic topics with which we'd been dealing.

He proved to be receptive and appreciative audience as we regaled him with stories about our tenure at Tom's cafe.

Lord knows waitresses meet some odd ducks over the years. Not all of them are out-of-towners coming in off the highway or seasonal tourists.

Tom's also boasts a crew of unusual regulars. The big round table in the front is permanently reserved for a rotating gang of locals who migrate in and out during the day according to their current need for caffeination.

Don't bother going to the CIA for intel. If you want the scoop on anything from politics to the latest divorce brewing in town, go to the round table.

Tori told us about training the new girls—primarily a matter of getting them used to Tom himself. Don't get me wrong, the guy is an absolutely wonderful boss when you get to know him. Unfortunately, he has one volume level—extreme.

To our surprise and delight, Chase joined in with hysterical accounts of his own brief stint as a short order cook during college.

"It paid the bills," he said self-deprecatingly. "But I knew it wasn't my calling in life. Every single time I had to yell 'order up,' I was terrified that everything on the plate was inedible. I'm probably the only person in the world who lost twenty pounds working as a cook."

I liked that he could laugh at himself. Humor should never be underestimated as a valuable asset in a boyfriend.

Although I intended for us to split the check, Chase insisted on picking up the bill. He said it was his way of welcoming us both to the town square.

Funny and a gentleman. He was racking up points all over the board.

Once again, Chase suggested we take a walk around the square after we left the pizzeria.

The fact that Pete's was the only eatery on the square made me even more enthusiastic about Tori's idea of converting a portion of the store into a coffee shop/espresso bar. I said as much as we strolled down the sidewalk.

"It wouldn't be only for tourists," I said. "Don't you think people on Main Street would like to come in and have morning coffee?"

"I do," Chase agreed. "The coffee shop across from the grocery closed down a couple of years ago when the old guy who ran it died. People have missed having someplace to hang out."

Tori chimed in enthusiastically. "I have a brilliant idea."

She's humble like that.

"Why don't we ask Mark to do the remodel for the coffee shop at the same time he's working on my place?" she asked.

"Is there really any reason to wait? He might give you a better rate for doing all the work at one time."

"That's what he did when he remodeled my place," Chase said. "Amity had him do a lot of work at the pottery shop at the same time. It worked out well because he had all of his crew on site and could rotate them out. We split the cost on some of the materials, and Mark supervised both jobs at once. He did so much running back and forth, Fiona said we ought to put a traffic light on the sidewalk to keep folks from getting run over."

I laughed. "That sounds like her. She had a wonderful sense of humor. I'm beginning to appreciate what a natural she was at running the store."

"How are you doing with it?" Chase asked.

"It was a good week," I said instead of "I learned to move things with my mind" or "I've been helping a ghost binge watch '80's sitcoms." I also didn't mention I suspected that both the store itself and the resident rodent outpaced me in the smarts department.

What I was discovering I liked most about being a business owner was the "owner" part. Even on a slow day, I could look around and know everything in the place was mine.

I missed some parts of working at Tom's, like seeing the regulars every day and taking part in the steady flow of information, but the shop belonged to me. Everything there was ripe with potential for the realization of my own ideas. Now Tori's fertile mind had been added to the mix. She was right. There was no reason to wait to add a coffee area or anything else. I was the boss.

Let me inject another bit of literary foreshadowing here. We may not get to it in this story, but I think it bears mentioning that I had not yet realized Myrtle was the one in charge. Failing to ask her opinion about my plans would prove to be a problem sooner than later.

At that moment, however, none of us had anything more pressing on our minds than leisurely strolling around the town square on a beautiful spring afternoon. I already regarded the square as a separate entity within Briar Hollow.

Something of a renaissance had been taking place on the square over the last several years. Almost all the old red brick buildings were either occupied or under renovation to house some new endeavor. The seasonal tourist traffic and a sense of renewed municipal pride motivated the changes. Locals spent more time downtown, which made the idea of a coffee shop with sandwiches and baked goods all the more appealing.

Some of the stores already stayed open on Friday and Saturday nights, the way they had in the 1930s and 1940s, or so George and Irma told me. According to them, old-timers talked about how much fun it had been to come to town, park their cars on the square, and visit with passersby on the sidewalk.

I liked that image. My mental "to do" list included joining the Chamber of Commerce and the Town Square Association. I didn't want the store to be a passive inheritance. I wanted to succeed.

Neither Tori nor I could remember if we'd ever told Aunt Fiona about our dream of running a business together, but we felt she gave us an incredible gift.

Three times around the square seemed to be about the norm for Chase. We once again parted at the door of my shop, but this time, I suppose because Tori was standing there, I only got a hug and a peck on the cheek.

Chase qualifies as an accomplished hugger, however, so I didn't consider the parting a downgrade.

Once inside, Tori and I adjourned to the storeroom to discuss what Sheriff Johnson told us about Beth.

Flopping down on the loveseat, Tori looked at me and said,

"Are you going to tell Beth that her mother is organizing her funeral, or am I going to tell her?"

Surely I hadn't heard that right.

"Are you volunteering?" I asked.

"No. Duh," she said. "Can't you recognize one of those facetious question things when you hear one?"

I laughed. That was more like it.

"How about *we* tell her?" I suggested.

"In that case, I think *we* should find out when the service is scheduled before we break the news."

Good point.

I walked out to the counter and retrieved the phone directory. All I could remember about the local funeral parlor was that it was named *J* something. Thankfully, as sections of the alphabet go, there were few locals whose last name started with *J*.

I dialed Jenkins Mortuary. I dialed the number only to be greeted with doleful music and assurances that my call was mattered to them. I remained on hold while they "attended to the needs of the currently bereaved."

I rolled my eyes and held the phone out so Tori could hear an organ playing, "*Nearer My God to Thee*." On the third verse, a man's voice came on the line. "Jenkins Mortuary," he said. "May I help you?"

"Yes," I said. "I was wondering if the service for Elizabeth Barlow had been scheduled?"

"It has," the man intoned mournfully. "Such a tragic loss."

Uh, yeah, during the Reagan administration.

"The services will be held Wednesday afternoon at three o'clock," the undertaker continued. "Given the long-term effect of this case on the community, I would suggest an early arrival. The service will be here in our chapel, and our seating is limited."

I thanked him and ended the call. "Sounds like Beth will get a standing-room-only funeral," I said.

"I have no doubt," Tori said. "Even thirty years after the fact, murder is juicy stuff."

Seriously bad choice of verbal imagery.

Steering the conversation in a slightly new direction, Tori asked, "What do you think about Mr. Warmth and Personality up at the campground being a suspect back in 1985?"

"I think it's entirely too convenient," I said. "Besides, I'm sure the authorities ruled out everyone who worked at the campground as persons of interest."

Listen to me with the crime talk. Persons of interest.

"You know what's bugging me?" Tori said.

"No, what?"

"If Aunt Fiona was a big deal witch, and she was interested in who killed Jane, why didn't she figure out the connection to Beth and catch the killer?"

I didn't want to be disloyal to my aunt, but the same question crossed my mind more than once.

"If Fiona would answer my calls," I said, "I'd ask that very thing. I'm getting nothing but dead air from her. Maybe Fiona didn't have the right set of powers to catch the killer."

Tori cocked her head to one side. "Does that mean you *do* have the right powers?"

Why did I feel like somebody had just looked at me and said, "*Luke, I am your father*?"

"Do *not* go there," I warned. "I am totally making this stuff up from one minute to the next."

"Fair enough," Tori said, "but there's something else I find interesting."

"And that would be?"

"That the old campground coot went to the trouble of paying for a lawsuit to protect a hickory tree. Both Beth and

Twenty-Five were buried at the base of hickory trees. What's the deal with hickory trees?"

I shrugged. "You've got me. Maybe it's a coincidence. There are hickory trees all over this part of the country."

"Maybe," she said, "but I'd like to know more about that lawsuit."

"Well, that's easy enough."

My laptop was lying on the coffee table. I opened the machine, and in a few keystrokes, located a series of stories about the well-publicized legal action of one Woodrow Evers against the regional power company.

Sheriff Johnson hadn't been kidding about how serious Evers was about that tree. So serious, he chained himself to the trunk at one heated juncture of the fight. The *Briar Hollow Banner* carried a front-page photograph of a much younger version of the man we encountered sitting resolutely on the ground, manacled to the hickory.

As I studied the photograph, I could see that the controversial tree sat roughly 200 yards from the party barn in the center of the campground. If I had my bearings right, the venerable hickory would have been to our left as we drove in. The longer I stared at the picture, the more determined I became to see that tree for myself.

Tori read my expression. "You want to go back out there, don't you?" she asked.

"Yes, I do," I said, warming to the idea forming in my mind. "If I can touch things and get visions, why couldn't I touch that tree and see if it has anything to do with Beth's disappearance?"

For once, Tori was the voice of caution.

"I don't know," she said reluctantly. "You heard what the Sheriff said. Mr. Evers has a bad habit of shooting at trespassers."

Dodging bullets was not part of my plan, but I was determined to get back on the land. Maybe I could use the fact that Fiona and Evers didn't like one another to my advantage.

In the south, there are predictable times when we take to the kitchen and prepare food. Death, for instance, initiates a frenzy of green bean casserole making and *Cool Whip* slathering. Baked goods, on the other hand, are an acceptable way to tender an apology.

“How about this,” I suggested. “What if I bake up one of my world-famous lemon pies, and take it out there tomorrow to apologize for trespassing on his land? That way, I can see if I'm right about the location of the hickory tree and maybe figure out how you and I can sneak back in when you’re here next weekend.”

“You mean when I’m here for the service on Wednesday,” she corrected me. “I've already texted Tom and told him I need that day off and that I’ll be in late on Thursday.”

Shaking my head ruefully, I said, “You know, girlfriend, we really have to get better hobbies. Lately, all we do is look for ghosts and hang out with dead people.

From the doorway, Beth said in a small voice, “What's wrong with dead people?”

Now there’s an opening line for a conversation if I ever heard one.

Chapter Twenty-Five

When we told Beth about her funeral, the only thing that registered with her was that her mother would be in attendance. As delicately as I could, I pointed out to the girl that she wouldn't actually be able to speak to her mom. Beth's reaction brought tears to my eyes.

"I know," she said, "but it's going to be good to see her again after so much time."

"Honey," I said gently, "do you realize that your mom may not look quite the way you remember her? She's thirty years older now."

Beth's brow crinkled, and then she said sweetly and a little brightly, "I guess that means she'll look more like Grandma now. Cool."

With that, she floated back out of the storeroom.

I looked at Tori and we both shook our heads. If we didn't find a way to help Beth, I didn't think either one of us would be able to stand it.

Tori couldn't put leaving off any longer. She had to get back to her place and face the work world the next day. She reluctantly got her things together, and I pushed her out the front door.

"You'll call me if anything comes up?" she asked, tossing her suitcase in the backseat of her car.

"Of course I'll call," I said. "We've talked to each other every day of our lives since we were in the first grade. You're the first one to hear everything. Quit worrying that you're going to miss out on something."

Tori got behind the wheel and then rolled the window down. Looking up at me with a serious expression, she said, "Jinksy, are you sure about this idea of taking a pie out to the campground tomorrow? I'm still worried it's a bad plan."

"I'm sure," I assured her.

Who in the world can turn down lemon pie?

The answer to that question would be Woodrow Evers.

The next morning, I spent an hour and a half in the kitchen making pie crust from scratch and cooking up the most beautiful lemon pie I'd made since I won a blue ribbon at the youth show my junior year in high school.

Aunt Fiona could hardly be described as a domestic goddess, but she nursed an affinity for plastic ware. I found a pie carrier in the cabinet, and once my creation cooled, I taped a sign on the front door. "Out for Errands. Be back in an hour."

The instant I drove into the campground, Evers charged out. I guess he recognized my Prius. In a state where big trucks are the norm, a hybrid sticks out like a sore thumb.

The old man stormed toward me, shouting orders for me to get off his land before he called the law. I hadn't even managed to offer him a civil good morning.

When he finally paused for breath, I said, as politely and patiently as I could manage, "Mr. Evers, I'm here to apologize for being rude and trespassing on your land yesterday."

He interrupted me immediately. "Your idea of apologizing

for trespassing is to trespass again, young lady?" he demanded with a derisive snort. "You really are related to Fiona Ryan, aren't you?"

Setting my jaw, but keeping the forced smile on my face, I tried again. "I don't mean to be trespassing, sir. I brought you a pie."

"I don't like pie," he snapped. "Now get the hell off my land."

From behind him, a voice said, "Now, Dad, that's not very neighborly."

Evers glanced over his shoulder and scowled. "W.J.," he said, "you need to learn to tend to your own business."

I looked past Evers and saw a man in his mid-forties walking toward us. Although he didn't have an athletic build, his tanned features indicated he spent a lot of time outdoors. There was a strong resemblance in his face to Evers, which led me to guess that "W.J." might stand for "Woodrow, Jr."

"Hi," I said to the newcomer. "I really am sorry to cause such a fuss. I wanted to apologize for trespassing yesterday."

W.J. gave me an open and genial smile. "I'm sorry for Dad's reaction," he said. "He doesn't like anyone but registered campers on the premises. He told me you drove through yesterday just to have a look around. I assured him you weren't here to do any harm then, and clearly, you're not now. That pie is beautiful."

"It's lemon," I ventured, trying to keep the thin line of communication open. "I baked it fresh this morning."

"Since you're related to Fiona Ryan," the old man growled, "I wouldn't be surprised if you put arsenic in the damn thing."

"Dad," W.J. said firmly, "that really is enough. Why don't you go on back to the office and let me talk with Miss Ryan?"

"It's Hamilton," I said. I shifted the pie container to my left hand and held out my right as the younger man leaned in for the handshake. “Jinx Hamilton,” I said, clarifying the introduction. “Fiona and my mother were sisters.”

He shook my hand with a firm grip. “W.J. Evers,” he said. “It’s a pleasure to meet you.”

Beside us, Woodrow cleared his throat and spit dismissively in the dirt at our feet. “I've had enough of this chit-chat,” he said. “You can stand out here yacking with white trash if you want to, boy, but I've got work to do.”

My mouth dropped. I wasn’t sure what was more shocking, the disgusting spitting or the fact that the old guy had the nerve to call me white trash. I watched with a dumbfounded expression on my face as he stalked off.

Before I could say anything, W.J. rushed to fill the void. “I am so incredibly sorry for my father’s utter lack of manners,” he said.

“I hope you'll excuse me for saying so,” I said, “but your father doesn't have much in the way of people skills.”

W.J. laughed. “No,” he agreed. “Nobody is ever going to describe Dad as warm and fuzzy.”

Since I didn’t know what else to do, I handed him the pie, which he accepted with a smile.

“Thank you for this,” he said. “I really mean that. If you're interested in camping with us, I'll speak with my father.”

Since the conversation was starting to take on that tone of polite pre-termination, I told a white lie. “I love to camp,” I said with faux enthusiasm. “The grounds here are so beautiful.”

I used the statement as an excuse to turn around in the spot and survey my surroundings. In the distance, down the slope and to the right of where I stood, I spotted the majestic hickory exactly where I expected it to be.

What I didn't expect was a small building that was obviously a recent addition to the compound. A tidy sign hanging from the eave said, "Museum." Perfect. I could use that to buy myself more time.

"You have a museum on the property?" I asked with interest. "What's in your collection?"

W.J. brightened considerably. "I specialize in Native American artifacts," he said. "Not just the tribes in this area, but also groups that extend up into New England and all the way to the border with Canada."

"Oh," I said, making the word sound breathy. "That's fascinating. Is there any chance you might show me?"

Yes, as much as I hate to admit it, I might have fluttered my eyelashes.

W.J. flushed with pleasure. "You're really interested?" he asked.

The way he posed the question, I suspected that even though his museum was smack in the middle of his property, he didn't get a lot of foot traffic through the front door.

"Oh, yes," I said. "I'm very interested."

This time, his response shifted into full-blown gallantry. "Then, of course, I'll give you a tour," he said. "It would be my pleasure."

I fell in beside him as we walked across the campground. The longer that I could keep him talking, the better chance I might have to learn something about his eccentric father.

"How in the world does your mom put up with your dad being so grouchy?" I asked.

W.J. answered in an almost hushed voice. "My mother died when I was 12 years old."

"I'm so very sorry," I said. "That was presumptuous of me to ask."

"No," he said, "not at all. I think Dad would be much better if she were still here to keep him company. She was the only person he got along with."

As we approached the small building, I said, "It must have

been hard for him to be out here raising you by himself all these years. What year did she die?"

"Nineteen-eighty-two," W.J. said. Then he added sadly, "I can't believe that she's been gone thirty-three years."

In my head, I did the math. In 1985, when Beth disappeared from the party, W.J. was 15 years old.

"Was this an interesting place to grow up?" I asked as he held the door of the building open for me.

"It was," he said. "When you run a campground, there are always new people to meet and watch during the season. The winters can get lonely, but otherwise, I've always liked the business."

"Are you here for a visit?" I asked.

"No." he said. "I've recently moved home. Dad is getting on up there in years. He needs more help than he's willing to admit or accept."

Something told me that was an understatement.

As W.J. finished his sentence, he flipped the light switch by the door and flooded the interior of the museum with brilliant light. I have to admit, I was immediately impressed. The collection appeared to be lovingly and meticulously curated. Antique display cases lined the walls, no doubt rescued from stores in the area. Many of them looked like the cabinets that filled my shop. The shelves contained perfectly aligned groupings of artifacts, all carefully labeled. As I took in more detail, I realized the cases were arranged in regional groupings, with individual cases dedicated to particular tribes.

"This is an incredible private collection," I said, and meant it.

"Thank you," he said. "I've been doing this since I was a boy. I saved my allowance to buy my first pieces. Many of the things in my collection now are of museum quality."

"What was your first artifact?" I asked.

"Oh," he said, giving me a boyish grin, "that's easy. It was a Seneca throwing tomahawk. I still have it. Let me show you."

He crossed the room, opened one of the cabinets, and took out a long-handled tomahawk. The head was slightly elongated with one broader, crooked end. The piece strongly resembled a modern hatchet, but it had clearly been worked by hand.

W.J. held the artifact out to me. "Hold it," he said encouragingly. "The balance the Seneca were able to achieve in their throwing tomahawks is a testament to the sophistication of their workmanship."

I didn't want to tell him that I wouldn't have been able to recognize balance in a tomahawk to save my life, but I took the weapon he held out to me.

That's when it happened. I should have known that touching an artifact that old would likely trigger a vision. Being so new to psychometry, I forgot to exercise the correct caution. The instant my hand touched the wood, the modern scene around me disappeared.

I was still looking at the Tomahawk in my hands, but now they were the hands of a young male. Moccasins encased my feet and I was bare-legged. The weight of a belt rested at my waist.

From somewhere in front of me, a girl's voice called out. Looking up, I saw a stormy sky. Off to my left I made out a strange light that didn't fit the rest of the picture. The illumination seemed oddly mechanical.

The girl spoke again. Squinting in the half-light, I tried to locate her, only to realize I was looking at Beth tied to the trunk of the hickory tree. She met my eyes directly, and said in a pleading voice, "Please, you don't have to do this."

The words echoed in my mind. Then the room righted itself and I was back in present time. W.J. looked at me with concern. "Are you okay?" he asked. "You were here with me one minute, and then you were gone."

"I'm so sorry," I stuttered. "Yes, uh, yes, I'm fine. I zone out like that sometimes when I get hungry. It's a blood sugar . . . thing. I skipped breakfast this morning. Bad idea."

It was a lame excuse, but in a pinch, blaming your blood sugar generally works. Or at least it always did with my mom, who, admittedly, can be a bit of a hypochondriac.

"Oh my goodness," he said, "do you need to sit down? Should I find you something to eat? Like a piece of candy?"

"No," I said, "but thank you. Really. I'm fine. I should be going anyway."

"Are you alright to drive?"

"I feel much better now," I said. "I need to get back to the store. I've been away too long. I don't have any help, you see. It's just me, so I had to close up this morning. I'll have something to eat when I get back."

"I'd be happy to follow you into town to make sure you get there okay," he said.

I declined his offer with more assurances that I would be fine and thanked him for showing me his collection. "Maybe I can come back sometime," I said, "and we can finish the tour."

"Anytime," W.J. said. "I'll make sure you get a more cordial reception from my father on your next visit."

Thankfully I didn't say what immediately popped into my head. *When pigs fly.*

W.J. walked me to my car and thanked me again for the pie.

As I drove away, I looked in the rearview mirror. He was watching me closely. I wondered if W.J., like his father on Saturday, wanted to make sure I really left the property.

At the time, however, I wasn't nearly as interested in understanding the motivations of the Evers men as I was in trying to figure out how in the world Beth managed to get herself killed by a Seneca Indian in 1985.

Chapter Twenty-Six

The store felt like an oasis of calm after my experience with the tomahawk. When I came in the door, Myrtle dimmed the lights, and a package of chamomile tea scooted to the edge of a shelf.

"It's that obvious, huh?" I said.

The lights dimmed again.

"Thanks Myrtle," I said. "But the tea will knock me out like a light. I'll have it tonight before I go to bed."

I carried the tea box with me into the storeroom to show Myrtle I appreciated her consideration. Rodney stuck his head out from between the liniment cans and wiggled his whiskers at me.

"Don't you start, too," I said. "I'm fine."

As if he needed proof, Rodney held out his paw and motioned me over. When I came close and put out my hand, he scampered up my arm and settled on my shoulder.

"Okay, okay," I said. "We can hang out."

I walked to the chair and sat down, taking out my phone to text Tori and let her know I was okay. My message didn't mention anything about the vision. Some things can't be described via thumb typing. I'd save that story for later when we talked.

Normal activities kept me occupied for the rest of the day. Beth hovered two steps behind me most of the time asking endless questions about her impending funeral.

The idea that her casket would hold nothing but bones bothered her.

"I mean," she said, "it's not like I'm going to be looking my best."

There you go. Conclusive proof. Vanity survives death.

"Honey, I'm sorry to tell you this," I said, "but nobody is going to be thinking about that, and they're certainly not going to be looking at you. You have to understand that the people who will be coming to the service won't be there for you. Funerals are for the living."

Oh, my God. Did I say that? I am turning into my mother.

Beth mulled over my statement with the same confused concentration she would have applied to one of those algebra equations where the value of X defies calculation.

"I don't know," she said finally. "Since I'm the dead person, I think it ought to be all about me."

Oddly enough, I found that a difficult point to argue.

When I related the conversation to Tori that night over Facetime, she burst out laughing. "God," she said, "Beth really was the head cheerleader, wasn't she?"

I giggled since I knew we were both thinking about Darla Sue Bumiller.

Yes, I know, her name was tragic, and she over-compensated in her quest to be "fabulous."

Darla Sue was our graduating class diva, whose crowning achievement in life, when last I saw her, was being named head cheerleader four years straight.

"Now, now," I said, struggling to regain my composure.

"We sound like the passably popular girls who hate the thoroughly popular girls."

"Well, duh," Tori said. "That's because we do."

"Tori," I said, in my best grown-up voice, "we're almost 30 years old. I think we can let old high school grudges go."

"For your information, I intend to remain 29 for life," Tori declared. "Besides that, you know as well as I do that we will still hate Darla Sue at our 50th reunion. Age has nothing to do with high standards."

Suppressing another giggle, I said, "Beth doesn't mean to be self-absorbed. She confided in me that she was killed before her senior prom. I think she's sees her funeral as her final big event."

"I'd say *death* was her last big event," Tori groaned. "At the hands of a completely out-of-place Native American swinging a scary hatchet thing."

"Out of place is right," I agreed. "That was the last thing I expected to see."

"Jinksy, you're going to have to be more careful about what you pick up," Tori said. "You really do *not* have this psychometry thing under control."

Gee. Ya think?

"I kind of do and I don't," I said defensively. "Here in the store, I can pick something up, sort of make my mind go blank, and get a vision."

"Yeah," Tori said, "but how about blocking a vision you don't want to have?"

"That I can't do," I said, "but in all seriousness, I'm not sure I could have stopped this one even if I tried. It was powerful. Whoever was holding the tomahawk was breathing hard. I could feel his heart pounding in my chest."

"Whoa," Tori said, "that's intense."

"You have no idea," I said. "I've been trying to get it out of my head all day."

"I don't blame you," she said, "and we should probably stop talking about it so you can get some sleep tonight. I'm going to work the breakfast shift, and then leave to drive over. The funeral is at three o'clock, right?"

"That's what the funeral director told me," I confirmed, "but let's get there early, so we can get a seat in the back."

"You want to get there early so we can get a seat in the back?" Tori said skeptically. "Don't you have that turned around?"

"Nope," I said. "We need to be able to watch everybody who comes to the service."

"Come on," Tori scoffed. "That would be way too easy. The killer isn't going to show up with a sign that says, 'I did it!'"

"I know," I said, "but I still want to get a good look at everyone who's there. Nothing we've learned so far, including the vision I had today, gets us any closer to finding out who killed Beth or figuring out if the same person killed Jane. At this point, I'll take any clue I can get."

We said our goodnights, and I quietly transferred Rodney, who had fallen asleep on my shoulder, to the soft confines of his nest box. He let out a cute rat snore but otherwise didn't move.

On my way up the stairs, I called out, "Night, Myrtle."

A soft chime answered me. I switched off the lights, and she turned them right back on again with a sound effect that sounded like maternal clucking.

"Don't trust me on the stairs?" I asked. "Okay, then turn them off for me when I get up there, okay?"

When I turned the doorknob to enter the vestibule the lights downstairs went off—and I didn't even have to do that "clap on, clap off" thing.

The pile of slumbering cats on the sofa woke up for their

bedtime snack, but Beth was nowhere to be seen. That didn't last.

The next morning, I awakened under the usual combined glare of four cats and an excited ghost concerned that we were going to be late for her "thing."

Blinking the sleep out of my eyes, I brought the clock into focus and stifled some very not-nice language. The cats had heard it all before, but I tried not to swear like a sailor in front of Beth. "Honey," I said with bleary patience, "your 'thing' isn't for another ten hours."

I swung my feet over the edge of the bed only to be greeted with Beth's shocked pronouncement, "Does your hair always look like that when you wake up?"

I glanced in the mirror and had to admit I was sporting an epic bed head. One or more of the cats must have "groomed" me in the night. I know that may sound gross to clueless non-cat people, but those of us in the know recognize a major feline compliment when we receive one.

Ignoring Beth's assessment of my appearance, I ran both hands through the tangled mess and achieved at least a semblance of order. We all went into the kitchen where the order of business was feed the cats so they'd shut up, make my coffee so I could wake up, and explain to Beth she needed to *not* talk to me before the sun was up.

"Oh," she said. "You're one of *those* people in the morning. Okay. See you downstairs. Bye."

If only living people could catch on and blink out.

The instant I walked downstairs at seven o'clock, Beth said, "You're not dressed for the funeral."

That would be the funeral that was now eight hours away.

When the bell on the front door jingled at 10:30 announcing Tori's arrival, I felt like the cavalry had arrived.

Beth greeted her with the same critical eye she applied to me. "You're wearing pants to my funeral?"

"Would you rather I go in my underwear?" Tori shot back.

If a ghost could blush, Beth would have turned beet red. Instead, her form wavered around the edges, which caused Tori to take pity on her.

"Fashions have changed in the last thirty years, sweetie," Tori said. "It's acceptable now for a woman to wear pants to a funeral."

"I don't know," Beth said doubtfully. "I was studying to be a Kappa Kappa Gamma and that doesn't sound right.

Studying to be a Kappa Kappa Gamma?

For those of you who have no clue what we're talking about, see *A Southern Belle Primer: Or Why Paris Hilton Will Never Be a Kappa Kappa Gamma* by Maryln Schwartz.

"Let me guess," Tori said. "You were a legacy."

"Well, yes," Beth admitted haltingly. "But they would have *wanted* me. Excuse me. I'm going to go check on the cats."

After I was sure she was gone, I turned to Tori, "Normally, I'd tell you that wasn't very nice, but since she was driving me insane with all this funeral talk, I wish you'd gotten here an hour earlier."

"Quickest way to shut up a would-be sorority girl," Tori grinned, "call her a legacy."

Over the next four hours, Beth popped in and out several times until she finally wore us down. We left for the funeral home at 2:15. Since it was a 5-minute drive, we not only nabbed seats in the back, we had the whole place to ourselves.

Beth instantly floated to the front of the room to evaluate the casket, which looked like something fit for Snow White. The box was sparkling white, with shiny silver handles, and pink roses entwined in a border around the lid. Banks of floral arrangements surrounded the casket, including a massive spray of red roses with a black banner bearing the words, "BHHS Class of 1985, We Will Never Forget."

Even though there was no one else in the chapel, Tori

leaned over and whispered, "If that bunch we were in school with sent flowers, the ribbon would say, 'Thank God and Greyhound she's gone.'"

Stifling a laugh, I channeled my mother and said, "Stop that. Be reverent."

That did nothing but set us both into a fit of suppressed giggling. Both moms routinely leveled that same admonishment to us in church when we were kids.

From the front of the room, Beth shot us a highly convincing glare of disapproval for a middle-aged teen. We hastily composed ourselves as other people began to filter into the chapel one and two at a time. Within thirty minutes, the service was indeed standing room only.

At three o'clock, the minister came down the aisle leading the pallbearers, who took their seats on the front row. I was surprised to see Chase with them, looking trim and handsome in his dark suit with a single white rosebud pinned to his lapel.

Once the men were in place, the funeral director escorted Emily Barlow to her seat. We all stood as the grieving woman passed. She was small with gray hair that still showed hints of a more youthful chestnut. As I watched her walk, I detected the suggestion of a limp. Chase did his work well with her shoes.

The minister held his hands up and motioned us back into our seats. That's when I saw Beth. She was standing directly in front of her mother, looking down at her with an expression so filled with love and longing, I felt a knot rise in my throat.

Apparently, Mrs. Barlow had no family, because she sat alone in the front pew—or at least she thought she was alone.

As the preacher began to speak, Beth sat down beside her mother. At the same time, Mrs. Barlow turned toward the empty space beside her.

Frowning slightly, she tentatively reached out. Her fingers touched Beth's chest, just where her heart would have been, and Beth's form grew stronger from the contact.

I don't know if her mother saw her, but a look of great peace settled over the woman's features as she turned her attention back to the sermon.

The minister refrained from using the circumstances of Beth's death to deliver some ponderous consideration of God's mysterious ways. Instead, he built his remarks around Matthew 19:14, "Jesus said, 'Let the little children come to me, and do not hinder them, for the kingdom of heaven belongs to such as these.'"

When he was done, a woman from the Methodist church sang, "*In the Garden.*" On the last verse, the undertaker directed the mourners out of the chapel one row at a time. We filed out with the rest, joining the silent crowd lining the walkway from the door to the hearse.

In a few minutes, the pallbearers appeared, walking slowly with Beth's casket. Mrs. Barlow followed behind Beth at her side.

On the way to the cemetery, I looked in the rearview mirror and saw a long line of cars with their headlights on. "Can you believe how many people came to the service?" I asked Tori.

She looked at me with red-rimmed eyes. "Do you think Mrs. Barlow knows Beth is with her?" she asked.

"I don't know," I said softly, "but I sure hope she does."

Once the casket was unloaded at the cemetery, Chase came to stand with Tori and me. He hugged us both briefly and during the prayer, he took hold of my hand, entwining our fingers.

When the brief service ended, we all stood in line to offer our condolences to Mrs. Barlow.

"I didn't know you'd be here," I said to Chase in a low voice. "We could have all come together."

"Emily called me last night," Chase said. "They were shy a

pallbearer. I was glad to help out even though I didn't know the girl."

As we approached, Mrs. Barlow, who had been sitting, stood to hug Chase. "Thank you so much for stepping in at the last minute," she said.

"I'm honored you asked me," he said. Turning slightly toward us, he added, "Emily, this is Jinx Hamilton and her friend, Tori Andrews. They're the ones who found Beth."

"Oh!" Mrs. Barlow said. "I'm so glad you're here. I was going to come to the store to talk to you." As she spoke, she engulfed me in a hug and whispered in my ear, "Thank you for giving me my little girl back."

From behind me, Beth whispered urgently, "Please tell her I'm glad to be home."

Still holding Emily Barlow close, I said, "I think she's glad to be back with you, too."

Without turning loose of me, Emily drew back and met my eyes. "You feel her, too?" she whispered. "You know that she's here?"

"Yes, ma'am," I said. "I do."

Chapter Twenty-Seven

As we started to walk away from the temporary canopy, Tori caught hold of my arm and discreetly pointed at the granite marker beside Beth's open grave. "*Donald Barlow, Beloved Husband and Father, 1940-1983*."

"That poor woman," Tori whispered. "She lost her husband two years before Beth was murdered. He was only 43 years old. That's awful."

Since Chase was walking with us, I couldn't very well bring up the point that Beth never mentioned her dad, which seemed strange.

"From what I've heard," Chase said, also keeping his voice low, "Don Barlow died of pancreatic cancer."

After watching her husband succumb to such an awful disease, I couldn't imagine how Emily Barlow kept her sanity when her daughter disappeared.

"Mrs. Barlow must be a strong woman," I said as we made our way to my car. That's when I noticed Colonel Longworth beckoning to me from his obelisk. I caught Tori's eye and nodded covertly in the vicinity of the marker.

She turned her head as unobtrusively as possible, and I saw her eyes widen. She saw the Colonel as well.

"Are you two headed back to the store?" Chase asked.

"Actually, no," Tori said. "I'm entering another online photo contest, so we're planning on exploring the cemetery."

"Well, I have to get back," Chase said, "but maybe we can all get together later?"

Tori and I had already agreed to spend the evening running down everything we knew about the murders, but I couldn't tell Chase that. "We're sort of planning a girl's night," I lied. "But how about breakfast? Tori makes a western omelet that's out of this world."

Chase's eyes brightened. "That would be great," he said. "And I haven't met your cats yet."

"Perfect," I said. "Come on over at eight, and we'll have the food ready. That way neither one of us will have to open up late."

As Chase walked away, I said to Tori under my breath, "That photo contest excuse comes in really handy."

"I know," she said, "and it's totally reusable."

We took our time threading over to Colonel Longworth. He seemed to get that we didn't want to be noticed and waited patiently for us.

"Hi, Beau," I said when we came within earshot.

"Ladies," he said, performing his usual bow. "The service was lovely."

"You were there?" I asked. "I didn't see you."

"The farther I wander from my marker during the day," he said, "the more insubstantial I become, but I thought circumstances behooved me to pay my respects."

Tori was going through the motions of taking photographs of his tombstone, an activity which seemed to interest the old soldier. "May I ask what you are doing with that device, young lady?" he said.

"I'm making it look like I'm taking pictures so anyone watching us won't think we're talking to thin air," she replied.

Longworth frowned. "I am familiar with the battlefield photographic work of Mr. Matthew Brady," he said, "but his equipment was more ponderous than what you are holding."

"Things have changed a bit since the 1860s," Tori said. "Here, let me show you."

She aimed the camera at Longworth, who was standing in front of his monument and snapped a picture. Then she walked over beside the old spirit and called the image up on the phone's screen.

She let out a gasp and gave me an astonished look.

"What?" I said.

"Come see for yourself," she answered.

When I looked at the image, I could make out a hazy corona in the vague shape of a man standing in front of the impressive marble obelisk.

"I would not say that is my best likeness," Colonel Longworth observed politely, "but I do appreciate the effort, Miss Tori."

Uh, yeah. Never mind that if we wanted to, we could go viral with that picture and probably make some money doing it. Which, in case you don't already know, we weren't going to do.

"Was there something you wanted to tell us, Beau?" I asked, remembering why we'd come over to speak with the Colonel in the first place.

"Yes," he said. "We have all been trying to offer dear Jane some degree of consolation after the upset of your last visit. I cannot tell you why, and I do not know if the information is of any use, but she seems to have developed a preoccupation with President Andrew Jackson of Tennessee."

Oh God. Please, no dead presidents in the mix unless their pictures are on spendable paper.

"What do you mean 'a preoccupation?'" I asked.

"She keeps repeating 'Old Hickory' over and over again," the Colonel said. "You may not be aware that 'Old Hickory" was President Jackson's nickname. I did not know the man personally, as he died in 1845, but my father had the privilege of Mr. Jackson's acquaintance."

There was no point in trying to explain the significance of hickory trees in relation to the murdered girls to Colonel Longworth. We thanked him for telling us about Jane and promised to come back to the cemetery at night as soon as we knew anything that would help her.

As we walked away, Tori said, "Again with the hickory trees? What the *what*?"

"I'd say our next round of research begins with that question," I replied.

We expected Beth to ride with us to the cemetery from the funeral home, but she stayed with her mother in the limo. As we approached the car now, however, the girl sat in the backseat waiting for us.

Tori and I climbed in and endured an awkward silence, which Beth finally broke. "My casket was pretty, wasn't it?" she asked in a small voice.

"Yes," I agreed, looking at her in the rearview mirror, "it was."

"Those roses on the lid were like the ones on the wallpaper in my bedroom," she said, sounding wistful. "Do you think my mom knew I was sitting with her?"

"I do," I told her. "Your mother told me she felt you with her at the service."

"Is that what she whispered to you when she hugged you?" Beth asked.

"Yes, it was."

"I wish I could hug her," Beth said, her voice catching. She was silent for a minute and then said, "My dad's service was at the same funeral home as mine."

"You've never talked to us about him," I ventured tentatively.

"I'm kind of mad at him," Beth admitted, staring out the window at the tombstones.

"About what?" Tori asked.

"Because he died," Beth said, "and because he didn't come find me and take me someplace better when I died."

Neither one of us knew how to respond to that, so I started the car and pulled away from the graveyard. After we drove a couple of blocks, Beth said, "Who were all those old people sitting there wearing the red-and-black ribbons?"

Oh boy. This was going to be fun.

"Those were the people in your graduating class," I said.

"*My* class?" Beth exclaimed. "But they looked like somebody's parents!"

"Honey, they probably are somebody's parents," Tori said. "If you were alive, you'd be 48 years old."

That idea threw Beth so completely for a conceptual loop, she didn't say another word all the way back to the store. Once we were inside, for the first time since she'd been with us, she instantly disappeared.

"Uh oh," Tori said. "I don't like that."

"Me either," I agreed. "Let's hope she comes back later."

We went upstairs and changed into more comfortable clothes before camping out in the storeroom with Rodney and our laptops. For the next couple of hours, we went at the hickory thing from every angle we could imagine, even trying to figure out if there really *was* some sort of Andrew Jackson-worshipping death cult running amok in the area.

Finally, I threw my hands up in disgust. "The hickory trees are a coincidence," I said. "We need to move on to something else."

All of a sudden, a small roundish object whizzed out of nowhere and hit me between the eyes.

"Hey!" I yelped, jumping up from my chair and rubbing my forehead. "What the heck was that?"

In a bid to be helpful, Rodney scampered under the sink and came out with a nut of some kind. Standing upright on his hind legs, he offered it to me. I took it, and Tori and I both bent down for a closer look.

"What is it?" she said, as Rodney scampered up my arm and joined our examination of the mystery object

Before I could answer, another one of the missiles careened toward me, but this time, Rodney was on the case. He made a brilliant leap from my shoulder, caught the projectile in mid-air, and executed a perfect three-point landing on top of Tori's head.

Tori looked at me with an expression that said, "do something."

I held out my hand and Rodney climbed into my palm, clutching another one of the nuts in his paw.

"Let's go out on the proverbial limb here," I said. "Myrtle, are these hickory nuts?"

The shop responded by sending down a veritable hickory nut shower.

"Okay, okay, stop!" I ordered. "We get it. The hickory thing isn't a coincidence, but could you give us something else to go on?"

At that request, an arrow winged past my nose and landed smack in the middle of the calendar on the far wall, skewering the image of Bart Simpson on the illustration.

Which was fine with me, because what the heck was Aunt Fiona doing with a Simpsons calendar anyway?

Being careful to put the important part first, I said, "Don't answer me with any more arrows, but are you trying to tell us there's a connection between the Indian thing and hickory trees?"

Myrtle threw a confetti shower of gold stars at us and blew on an invisible party horn. Apparently, the teacher was pleased.

"Well, okay then," Tori said. "Back to square one. Indians and hickory trees."

It took us until almost two o'clock in the morning to find the answer. Tori was half asleep on the loveseat, but I was reading an article about Seneca Indian mythology when a single phrase jumped off the page: "bringing the dead to life."

"Tori," I said, "wake up. You have to hear this."

"Huh? What?" she said, sitting up blinking and trying to get her eyes to focus. "You find something?"

"Listen to this," I said, reading from the screen of my computer. "'In the mythology of the Seneca people, the hickory tree plays a prominent role in tales associated with bringing the dead back to life. In a series of well-recorded stories, the bones of the deceased are placed at the base of a large hickory tree, often after the flesh has been consumed by cannibals.'"

"Cannibals?!" Tori said, now fully awake.

"Hold on," I said. "There's more. 'The person who positions the bones attempts to resurrect the deceased by pushing them against the tree while commanding the departed to rise. If the departed does not rise from the dead, the tree will fall, crushing their bones to dust, ending any chance they have for a second life.'"

"So, you think some Seneca Indian tried to kill Beth to see if he could bring her back to life?" Tori asked.

"No," I said. "I think someone obsessed with Seneca Indians tried to perform the resurrection ritual."

"Who?" Tori asked.

"Woodrow Evers, Jr."

Chapter Twenty-Eight

I was now more determined than ever to sneak onto the Briar Hollow Family Campground. I'd thought a great deal about my tomahawk-inspired vision and developed a working theory, which I now explained to Tori.

"If I could see Beth tied to the tree while I held the tomahawk," I said, "I should be able to see the same scene from Beth's perspective if I touch the tree."

"Which means you could see her killer," Tori said.

"Exactly."

"And we take this as proof to the authorities how?" Tori asked.

"That I don't know," I admitted. "First, I think we have to find out if W.J. really did it."

"Well," Tori said, "it's 2:00 a.m. and we're both beat, plus we have a hot guy coming for breakfast at eight o'clock. I say we call it quits for tonight. I'll tell Tom I have to stay an extra day, and we can sneak into the campground tomorrow night."

"Tom is not going to be happy," I warned.

"When is Tom ever happy?" she countered. "Besides, the

new girls are doing fine. I texted them when we got back from the funeral, and they both sent me thumbs up emojis."

Way better than smiling pile of poop guy.

I think we were both asleep before our heads hit the pillow —or in Tori's case, the sofa. That didn't keep us from being up bright and early; me, to feed the cats and her, to start cooking.

At about ten minutes of eight, a strange banging filled the kitchen. Tori and I both jumped, and then I started laughing.

"What's so funny?" Tori asked. "It sounds like the building is falling down."

"That's Chase," I said, reaching for a heavy wooden spoon. I used it to beat out a response on the pipes in the corner of the kitchen, which was promptly answered with more banging from the other side of the wall.

"That means he's coming over now," I said. "I'll go downstairs and let him in."

The instant my foot hit the stair, Myrtle turned the shop lights on. I was getting used to the home automation thing.

Chase was waiting for me at the front door. "Hey!" he said happily. "You figured out the jungle telegraph."

"I did," I said, laughing and accepting a good morning hug. "Come on upstairs."

He followed me into the apartment and was instantly the subject of wary appraisal from the ZYXW squad. Chase laughed when I explained about the names and sat down in the middle of the living room rug, waiting patiently until the cats came to him. In less than two minutes, Yule was upside down in Chase's lap getting his tummy rubbed, and Xavier was draped around his neck.

"Looks like I pass the background check," Chase said, grinning from ear to ear.

This guy really does like cats. Major check mark in the plus column.

Tori came out into the living room with a cup of coffee,

which Chase accepted with one hand while continuing to pet cats with the other. "Good morning," she said. "Are you hungry?"

"Starved," he said, "and whatever you're cooking in there smells fantastic."

"Does that mean you want a three-egg omelet or four?" Tori asked with a grin.

"Four," he said firmly. "Definitely four. I like round numbers."

Disentangling himself from the cats, Chase came into the kitchen, and the three of us talked while Tori finished cooking breakfast. We all agreed the service the day before was heart-wrenching but gave Mrs. Barlow a degree of closure she needed.

"Did you get some good pictures for your contest?" Chase asked Tori.

"I did," she said. "Would you like to see?"

To my considerable horror, she opened the photo of Colonel Longworth on her phone and handed it to Chase. His eyes widened as he studied the screen. "If I didn't know better, I'd say there's the ghost of a man standing there," he finally admitted.

"That's what I thought, too," Tori said, "but it's a corona created by the sun. Pretty cool though, huh?"

"It sure is," Chase said, handing her the phone back.

I shot her a look that plainly said "knock it off," before changing the subject. "We've officially hired Mark to do the expansion and renovation. Be prepared to start giving up your nights and weekends starting in about ten days."

Chase fairly beamed. "I can't wait!" he said. "It's going to be fun working on the project. I love having you . . . both for neighbors."

Tori and I heard the slight hesitation before the word "both."

Busted.

He *was* helping out to spend more time with me.

Suddenly, the day looked a whole lot better, even if we did plan to commit criminal trespass after sundown.

After Chase left, Tori called Tom, holding the phone away from her ear when he lost his mind about her taking another day off. She let him have his fit, and then pointed out if he was that unhappy with her, she could leave three weeks early. That shut his tirade down to a few muttered assurances that her pay would be docked.

With that chore done, we went downstairs and opened the shop. A few customers filtered in during the morning, but we had plenty of free time to contemplate the redesign of the first floor.

Tori took measurements, and we agreed a small booth and counter could be created in the square space between the stairs and the store's east wall. It would require the relocation of one set of floor-to-ceiling cabinets, which could be moved to the other side of the building.

We made notes and rough sketches to show Mark before breaking for lunch. Instead of worrying about cooking, Tori ran down to the grocery and came back with sandwich fixings.

"Irma and George are great!" she announced happily as she came in the door. "I love that they're right here on the town square."

Beth still hadn't returned, which concerned us both. I tried calling out to her a few times, but with no success.

"Myrtle," I said, "is Beth okay?"

The store answered with a sad sigh.

"Okay," I said, "but tell her we miss her."

Tori and I went into the storeroom, and to my great amusement, Tori took a hunk of Stilton cheese out of the sack and handed it to Rodney.

"*Stilton*?" I said. "Did you get him pears and a nice white wine to go with it?"

"I will if he wants me to," Tori cooed, smoothing the sleek fur between Rodney's ears.

Rodney had the good taste to bashfully duck his head as if the adulation was unwarranted, but he gobbled up the attention, right along with the expensive cheese.

"Okay," I said, as I spread mayo on bread, "do we need to take anything with us tonight?"

"I don't know," Tori said. "How are you figuring this is going to work?"

"When we drove by the campground the first time, I noticed a rest area about half a mile down the road," I said. We park there, walk along the road until we're up even with the gate, and then go over the fence."

"Walk," Tori said flatly. "For half a mile."

"Yes," I said, "walk. It's not like we can leave the car by the campground entrance."

She made a grumbling noise in the back of her throat but grudgingly admitted, "I guess you're right. So, flashlights if we're wandering around in the dark?"

"Definitely," I said. "Other than that, all we need to do is get me close enough to touch the tree."

"You're sure you can find it in the dark?"

"Yes," I said. "I got a good look at it when I was out there the other day."

"And what if Mr. Evers has motion-controlled cameras or something guarding the property?"

I hadn't thought about that.

"In that case," I said, "we're totally screwed."

"No," Tori said, arranging sliced tomatoes on roast beef, "we're *totally* screwed if he has guard dogs and motion-controlled machine guns."

"Have I ever told you how much I love that optimistic streak of yours?" I asked sardonically.

"Realistic," she said, finishing her sandwich assembly and taking a bite. She chewed the mouthful rhythmically, swallowed, and then said, "For the record, if there are big Rottweilers, it's every BFF for herself."

You know what they say. You don't have to run faster than the bear to get away; you just have to run faster than the guy next to you.

"You so would not do that to me," I said with conviction.

"Probably not," Tori said, "but if I get bit in the backside, you are going to be hearing about it for the next fifty years."

On second thought, maybe getting thrown to the dogs wasn't such a bad option after all.

Chapter Twenty-Nine

"You didn't tell me there would be bugs out here," Tori hissed, slapping at her neck. "You know I do not *do* bugs."

"You've been all over the mountains with your grandmother. You didn't care about bugs then."

"I didn't care about them because bugs never came around Granny Mo."

"That's ridiculous."

"It's also true."

"Tori, we're *outside*," I hissed. "Bugs live outside. We are technically in their house. They have the *right* to bite us."

"What are you, a lawyer for the Insect Civil Liberties Union?"

"Would you hush! This is supposed to be a stealth operation."

"Are you sure you don't have some magic insect-repelling power you haven't discovered yet?"

"*Hush*!"

This back and forth went on for a quarter of a mile. The

instant Tori stepped out of the car, which we parked in the rest area, the mosquitos targeted her as their blood bank du jour.

I, on the other hand, was so slathered down with anti-bug chemicals I could have been a walking citronella candle.

We both dressed in dark clothing and carried small LED flashlights, but for the most part we stuck to the shoulder of the road as our guide. We didn't see a single car, which helped and bolstered our confidence that we could pull our excursion off undetected.

On Saturday, the campground appeared filled to near capacity, but this was a Thursday night and school wouldn't be out for the summer for another two or three weeks. Plus, it was almost midnight. The only people likely to be in mobile residence were retirees, who I hoped had already turned in for the night.

As we drew closer to the main entrance, Tori quieted down, either because the mosquitos stopped torturing her or because she was too nervous to care anymore. I couldn't make out any lights through the trees, which was a good sign, and no man-made sounds disturbed the night.

After Tori brought up the possibility of electronic surveillance equipment at the gate, we agreed to look for telltale indicator lights, power cables, or suspicious boxes mounted on the posts or trees. When we found none of those things, Tori looked at me, pointed toward the gate, and mimed going over with a questioning look.

I nodded and climbed over first. If we got nailed by a blinding spotlight or set off a warning klaxon, the blame should fall squarely on me. For a reluctant second I sat on the top rail, then lightly dropped to the ground and waited for the worst. Nothing happened.

Tori scrambled over and joined me. We were now officially breaking the law, something neither one of us had done since high school, when firecrackers and a knothole in a tree were involved.

The driveway was smooth enough that even in the dim moonlight, we walked with confidence. Low clouds scudded overhead, making the limited illumination uneven at best. Still, we made slow but steady progress. Thankfully our eyes were completely adjusted to the darkness after the walk from the rest area.

When I could make out the dim outline of the central building, I put my hand on Tori's arm. Leaning in, I whispered, "We have to get off the road now. The tree is off to the left here. The ground is grassy, but I don't know how smooth it is, so be careful. Stick close to me."

"You don't have to worry about that," Tori whispered back. "I'm stuck to you like glue."

Our pace slowed over the unpredictable terrain. In daylight, the walk might have taken ten minutes, but at least half an hour passed before we came upon a massive hickory tree. I can't tell you how I knew, but I was certain we'd reached our destination.

I stopped Tori again with my hand.

"This is it?" she asked softly.

"Yes."

"You're sure?"

"Positive," I said.

"Now what?"

What did she mean, "now what?" We only came out here for one reason.

"I touch the tree," I answered.

When I said it, I started forward, but this time Tori put a restraining hand on my arm. "You don't know what's going to happen, Jinksy. I don't like this."

Now was a heck of a time to be having second thoughts.

"If I get in trouble, pull me off the tree."

"How will I know if you're in trouble?"

Just then, the moon broke through the clouds. I looked at Tori, really looked at her, and said from the heart, "You'll know. I trust you."

In the dim light, Tori smiled at me lovingly. "Okay, kiddo," she whispered. "Do your thing."

For the record, I don't just trust Tori with my life, I trust her with my *cats'* lives. That's how close we are.

That night, I didn't have to tell her that my heart was hammering in my chest or that I was sweating bullets.

She didn't have to tell me that she was in much the same condition.

We each knew the other was scared, but I was the one getting ready to use a barely controlled magical power to explore a potential murder site.

I don't think I would have even considered trying that without Tori there.

Together we always have the courage to do what we don't believe we can do alone.

That's another kind of magic. It's called friendship.

As I stepped forward, hands outstretched, I realized this was the first time I was intentionally going in search of a bad memory. That's what I was thinking about—to the complete exclusion of something so obvious to me now, I can't believe how clueless I was at that critical moment.

Trees are alive.

The tree reached for me at the same time I reached for it.

The point where we met wasn't exactly a joining of minds, but an ancient awareness surged through me. It wasn't only the life of *this* tree, rooted in this spot. There were other lives there with us—the tree that seeded this one, and all the trees that came before it. The line stretched back to a primordial world where this life form had no name, it just *was*.

With that flooding awareness came a deeply felt dignity

that resonated with me like a flavor. With it came the taste of sadness and the residue of lingering anger. The spirit of the tree felt aggrieved and dishonored. The slow thrumming of its sap fused with my bloodstream and drove me to follow my instinct and dive deeper into this alien sentience.

Until this joining, my power had been nothing but a parlor trick pulling memories out of hats. Now my heart took a true leap of faith. With complete conviction, I knew the tree meant me no harm. Drawing my thoughts together, I sent a request deep into the life pulsating under my hands. "Tell me."

I felt drawn into the tree's protective embrace as a single word echoed in my mind. "Watch."

Layers of time peeled away in the passing of seasons and the moods of the weather. There was the heat of lazy summer and the bite of icy winter, the wash of torrential rain and the tearing force of the wind. Then we arrived, on a night much like this one, under scudding clouds and transient moonlight, to a time when tight ropes cut into the hickory's bark, telegraphing the frantic vibrations of a trapped girl's struggles to free herself.

Without warning, a second awareness filled me. I relived the last moments of Beth's life. The bindings cut into my straining flesh. My lungs burned from the effort to escape until my head dropped to my chest in weary defeat. It was only then, as I watched shadows dancing on the ground, that I realized the flickering light wasn't coming from the moon.

Summoning all my willpower, I looked up. A video camera mounted on a tripod and outfitted with some kind of night-vision light faced the tree. Then I saw him, a young boy, barely a teenager, dressed in a native loincloth and clutching a tomahawk.

"Please stop fighting it," the boy said. "This will hurt, but not for long, and then I'll bring you back."

Sick panic and dread turned my stomach sour. I spoke, but Beth's voice escaped my dry lips and parched throat.

"Please. You don't have to do this. Just let me go. I won't tell anyone. I promise."

The words seemed to puzzle the boy. "But I have to do this," he said. "This is the only way I can bring her back."

With that cryptic phrase, he raised the tomahawk and started forward.

A surge of adrenaline rushed through me as I strained one final time against the ropes. One of the knots gave way, and I frantically struggled free of the cords. My limbs, numb from being bound, failed me, and I hit the ground hard, but I didn't stay there.

A sharp rock cut into the palm of my right hand. The pain focused me, bringing me to my feet and propelling me away from my attacker. The boy struck out with the tomahawk, but I deflected the blow, careless of the hot blood now coursing down my arm from the weapon's cutting edge.

The boy reacted wildly, grabbing for me to drag me back, tie me down, kill me. We knocked the video camera over, the camera itself shattering and falling away from the base. On instinct, the boy snatched up the tripod, swung it in a wide arc, and smashed it into my skull. The reverberation deafened me at the same time a sickening blackness drew me down into a gulf from which there was no return.

Beth's voice was there, but so was Twenty-Five's and Jane's, and other voices I didn't recognize, all howling in anguish. They'd all died right here on this spot.

No one had been there to save them from that black void, but I had Tori.

At that instant, she pulled me away from the tree. We both fell backward, but Tori absorbed the impact with her body, holding me in a tight and protective embrace. As if from a great distance, I heard her calling me.

"Jinx," she commanded. "Wake up."

When I didn't respond, she resorted to using my mother's voice. "Norma Jean Hamilton, you mind me."

I woke up.

Looking up at her, I said weakly, "You don't have to go all Kelly on me."

Tears welled in her eyes. "And you don't have to scare the living daylights out of me."

My senses were still tied to the tree's awareness of its world. I felt him before I heard him.

"Tori," I said softly. "We're not alone out here."

"No, you're not," a man said.

Turning my head, I looked up into the face of W.J. Evers—and into the barrel of the pistol he held in his hand.

"It would appear we have a problem," he said pleasantly. "You see, it's almost time to try again. I can't let you call attention to this place."

Tori's hand tightened on mine. The message in her eyes was clear. "Take him."

She knew I could protect us with my powers before I realized it myself.

I telegraphed, "*Not yet,*" before turning my attention back to W.J. "You can't get away with this."

"Oh, but I can," he said. "Now get up. Don't try anything."

As we stood up, W.J. ordered us to move closer to the tree. I was careful not to touch the bark, but I could still feel the hickory's presence in my mind.

"You don't have to do this," I said.

"That's so interesting," he said, sounding oddly academic. "Do you know that every single one of them has said those exact words?"

"How many of them have there been?" I asked.

"Six," he said. "One every five years since the first. One of you will be the seventh."

The next question was equal parts curiosity and a real desire to know.

"Why do you do it?" I asked.

"To bring her back, of course," he said. "But if it works this time, you'll come back, too. Try not to be too concerned. I think I understand how to do it correctly now."

From the darkness to our right, another voice said, "No, boy, you don't. This stops now."

Woodrow Evers walked out of the night and faced his son holding a double-barreled shotgun in his hands.

"You don't mean that Dad," W.J. said, his voice taking on a childish note. "I can bring Mom back, just like the Seneca legend says."

The moonlight carved deep ridges in the older man's face. "I protected you when you killed the Barlow girl," Woodrow said his voice breaking. "You were just a boy, obsessed with made-up stories, grieving for your mama. I couldn't lose you, too, so I protected you. Took you to doctors. Tried to find someone who could help you. I sent you to that boarding school and then off to college, but what did you do? You kept up this nonsense about Indians and raising the dead even after you failed time and time again. You spent my money to get a degree in the damned stuff and went right on killing."

W.J.'s face took on a defiant arrogance. "I was studying, accessing the wisdom of my people, and finding my personal magic. I am a highly regarded expert in my field."

Woodrow spat out his next words. "You're a highly regarded lunatic," he snapped. "There's no such thing as magic in this sorry world. You're born, you work your whole life, and you die. Your mama died, boy. She was an ordinary woman and she died."

A roar of rage rose from W.J.'s throat. He raised the pistol and fired at his father. The bullet struck the old man in the shoulder, but not before his father pulled both triggers.

The blast echoed through the trees, lifting W.J. off his feet and throwing him backward. He landed sprawled on the ground, blood pouring from a gaping wound in his chest.

I don't know why, but I went to him, kneeling on the ground and taking his hand.

As the pleading light died in his eyes, W.J. Evers whispered, "It would have worked this time. Mama's tree would have made it work."

Chapter Thirty

Sheriff John Johnson scratched his chin and looked at me skeptically. "Tell me again what you two were doing out here in the middle of the night?"

Tori and I opted to tell a hybridized version of the truth. "We got interested in the unsolved murder case when we found Elizabeth Barlow's bones," I said. "When I talked to W.J. Evers, I thought he sounded suspicious. We were trying to get a better look at the things in his museum to see if any of them could have been the murder weapon."

Under normal circumstances, no one would have bought a story that full of holes, but Woodrow Evers had already confessed to everything, so the Sheriff was willing to let our role in the night's events slide.

After Woodrow shot his son, the old man sat down on the ground and simply said, "One of you girls should call the police."

When the Sheriff arrived, Evers waived his rights and refused medical attention. "Bullet went clean through," he said. "I won't bleed to death in the time it takes me to tell you this story. Here is the only place I'll tell it. One time. Listen to me now, because I won't say another word once you take me off this land. I want those two young women to hear what I have to say, too. They earned that. They were idiots for coming out here, but doing it took guts, and I respect that."

The Sheriff agreed that we could witness Evers's statement, but only if we kept our mouths shut. The story the old man told proved to be so shocking, silence wasn't a problem on our part.

"W.J. never got over his mama's death," Woodrow said, speaking into the video camera a deputy set up in the campground office to record his statement. "He was in Boy Scouts and did a merit badge on Indian stuff. He got all obsessed with myths and legends. I never should have let him buy that damned tomahawk. It wasn't even made around here. Next thing I know, all W.J. can talk about is Seneca Indians and how they thought people could be brought back from the dead. That's what all this was about."

The Seneca myth referred to the bones of the dead person. According to his father, W.J. wanted to find out if the ritual would work before he dug his mother up. "He got it in his head that he had to kill them right there at the tree," Evers said. "You see, that's where it happened. My wife had an aneurysm in her brain. We didn't know about it. She and W.J. were down there at the hickory when that thing burst. She dropped dead right in front of him."

Woodrow described the night, three years after his wife's death, when he came upon W.J. dressed in native clothing standing over Beth Barlow's body. "He was just a boy," Evers explained. "It would have destroyed his life. Nothing was going to bring that girl back. I cleaned everything up and carried the body up to Weber's Gap. W.J. begged me to bury her at the base of a hickory tree. It was nonsense, but I did it for my son. I thought it was all over and done with."

Then, five years later, when W.J. was in college, he

kidnapped a woman off the streets and brought her to the campground. "I don't know who she was," Evers said. "She looked like she might have been a runaway, maybe a call girl. W.J. never told me if she had a name. I didn't even know they were on the property until I heard her yelling at him. It was the off-season. No one was here. I carried the body farther away this time. Put her at the base of another damned hickory tree, just like the first one."

By the third girl, the one the town knew as Jane Doe, the old man was covering for both W.J. and himself. Woodrow knew he was complicit in the crimes, but he refused to turn his son over to the law. "Other than Elizabeth Barlow, none of those girls had any significance to me," he said.

God. No wonder W.J. turned out the way he did.

"I messed that third one up," Woodrow said contemplatively. "I picked the wrong time to try to get rid of the body and almost got caught. I had to leave her out there on the trail in the open. That's when the whole town took her on as some kind of cause. I had a talk with W.J. and told him there couldn't be any more body dumps, but that didn't stop him."

With the same dispassionate tone, Evers described three more murders. "He brought them all here and killed them down there at the hickory tree. It worked out better for me, and I thought doing it all here was actually good. It should have gotten the whole resurrection idea out of the boy's head because I played along with that fourth one. If it was going to work, it would have worked then with me supervising everything so the idiot wouldn't screw it up."

Would have *worked*? Dear God. They were both crazy.

"We let some time pass," Evers said, "and then dug up the bones so W.J. could do his mumbo jumbo. He always insisted on videotaping everything. The tapes are all locked up in the safe there. I'll give you the combination so you can watch them."

We were *so* not going to that viewing party.

"Of course, the damned spell, or whatever he called it, didn't work," Evers went on. "We reburied the girl, and then I will be damned if W.J. didn't go off and get himself another degree in Indian lore. Next thing I know, he's here with another girl, going on and on about how he's finally figured out what he was doing wrong. We went through the whole thing again, and that one stayed just as dead as the others."

Evers turned to me. "It was about that time that your aunt started to be a problem," he snapped. "She was as bad as the rest of the town about trying to figure out who that third girl was, the one they all called Jane Doe. There wasn't one shred of proof linking that girl to us or to this place, but Fiona came snooping around anyway. She came right out and told me she felt evil on this land and warned me it was all going to come out one way or another. Even tried to help the electric company cut my tree down. Guess we showed her. The old bat dropped dead before we got caught."

You have no idea how much I wanted to tell him that Aunt Fiona might be dead, but she sent in the B-team to get the job done anyway.

"After the last girl, five years ago, I told W.J. it was time to give up. He agreed," Evers said. "She was one of his students up at the community college in Sparta. It was getting too risky. I didn't know he was planning on trying again until I heard him say it tonight. I didn't go down there to kill my boy. I saw you two skulking around in the dark and was going to scare you off with my shotgun. Then I heard what W.J. said and I snapped. I'm an old man. I'm tired of digging graves."

The *digging* made him snap. Some conscience.

"I'll show you where you can find the others," he said. "The belongings we took off all of them are up in my attic. You can have all that, too. That's it. I'm done talking."

As we watched, deputies escorted the old man out in handcuffs.

"What will happen to him now?" I asked Sheriff Johnson.

"First, he's going to the hospital whether he likes it or not," the Sheriff answered. "Then he's going to prison for whatever's left of his miserable life."

Johnson drove us back to my car and let us out with a stern admonition to stay out of trouble. Dawn was breaking as we drove into town and went into the shop. Beth was waiting for us.

"What happened?" she said. "I had the most awful dreams."

Ghosts dream?

"About what?" I asked, but I knew the answer.

"The night that crazy boy in the Indian costume killed me," she said. "He was the campground owner's son, wasn't he?"

"He was," I said. "Do you want to know why he killed you?"

"Yes, please."

We all went into the storeroom. Tori made coffee, and I told Beth the story. When I was done, she looked at me plaintively. "Now what do I do?"

"What do you want to do?" I asked.

Without hesitation, she said, "I want to go where my dad is."

As I started to tell her I'd try to help her, a strange light filled the room. By the door, the form of a tall man came into focus. Beth flung herself into his arms. "Daddy!" she cried joyously.

Don Barlow closed his eyes as he held his daughter close. When he opened them, he gave me a look of such gratitude, tears started to run down my cheeks. "Thank you for helping my baby girl," he said, in a rich baritone. "I'll take it from here."

They started to fade, and then Beth said, "Wait!"

Turning to me, she said, "Thank you for letting me stay with you. It was fun. Will you tell the cats I'm going to miss them?"

"I'll tell them, honey," I said, my voice thick with emotion.

"I'm going to miss you, too," Beth said. "You're going to like having Tori here. And that nice man next door? He really likes you."

"How do you know that?" I asked, smiling through my tears.

"Duh," she said mischievously. "What's the point of being able to walk through walls if you don't do it sometimes? He talks to Festus about you."

I laughed. "What does Festus say?"

"He likes you, too, and so do I. Can I come back and see you?"

"You can come back anytime," I said, "but I think you're going to be too happy where you're going to be worried about what we're doing."

"Will you help Jane now?" Beth asked.

"I'm sure going to try," I said. "Now go on with your dad, honey."

As Tori and I watched, father and daughter disappeared, and the room returned to normal.

"Wow," Tori said. "That's all I've got. Just *wow*."

I couldn't have said it better myself.

Chapter Thirty-One

Late Saturday afternoon, Sheriff Johnson walked in the front door of the store. Chase, Tori, and I were all sitting in the storeroom talking, so we invited the Sheriff to join us. I stifled a giggle when Rodney discreetly disappeared between his liniment cans.

"I wanted you to know that all of the girls have been identified except the one Evers thinks was a runaway," he said.

Twenty-Five. She said she was taken because no one knew her name.

"Who was Jane Doe?" Chase asked.

"A young kid from Oklahoma City, Susie Miller," the Sheriff said. "She was working her way across the country trying to get up to New York City. Had her heart set on being a model. She worked at the campground for a few days after Fiona saw her here in town. Evers hired Susie to clean the bathrooms and the big party barn. W.J. killed her when he was home from graduate school one weekend. I honestly don't think the old man even remembered he knew her."

Chase shook his head. He'd been none too thrilled when he

found out we went to the campground. "You could have told me," he said, sounding hurt. "I would have helped you."

Now, listening to the Sheriff, Chase said, for at least the tenth time, "It's a wonder that crazy old coot didn't kill you both."

"Amen to that," Johnson agreed, fixing me and Tori with a stern look. "I assume we're not going to have any repeat incidents of this sort of behavior."

"No, sir," I said, holding up my hand as if taking an oath. "My amateur sleuthing days are over.

Yeah. Famous last words.

It took a couple of weeks, but the Town Square Association raised the money to buy Jane a new tombstone. The night after it was put in place, Tori and I went to the cemetery. We found the ghost standing there looking down at the granite slab with a joyful look on her face.

As we approached, she turned toward us and said, "My name is Susie Miller."

"Hi, Susie," I said. "Do you like your new marker?"

"It's beautiful," the girl said. "It has my real name on it."

The Sheriff did everything possible to locate Susie's relatives, but her parents were both dead and there was no extended family. She really did belong to Briar Hollow now, so in Briar Hollow she would stay.

Colonel Longworth joined us at Susie's grave. "Miss Jinx, Miss Tori," he said, "would you do me the honor of walking with me?"

We fell in beside him, and once we were out of Susie's range of hearing, Beau said, "The others have asked me to convey their thanks to you. Young Susie is quite happy now that she knows her identity. Although she, like the rest of us, cannot leave this place, she is at peace for the first time since her life was taken. You have performed a great kindness for her."

I appreciated what he said and told him so, but the trapped state of the cemetery spirits bothered me. I had no answer for them. I planned to honor Aunt Fiona's tradition of keeping them company, but I wanted to find a way to give the ghosts the same freedom to choose that liberated Beth.

One loose end to the whole business could not be tied up, however—Twenty-Five. Earlier in the day, Tori and I returned to the clearing where her bones were discovered and once again encountered the angry spirit.

"Did you bring my body back?" the girl demanded, hovering menacingly in front of us.

"I told you last time that we didn't take your body," I said, holding up my hand in warning when her form started to pulsate. "Hold it right there. No more of your tantrums. We came here to tell you that the man who killed you is dead. His accomplice is going to prison for a long time. I'm sorry, but we still don't know your name or how to get in touch with your family."

"I told you," the girl said fiercely, "I was *somebody*."

"I know you were," I said.

"But you won't give me my body back," she snarled.

"That's not in my power to do," I explained.

"Then you're as worthless as the rest of them," the girl said. Around us, that same chill wind picked up strength sending the dust swirling at our feet. When the wind died away, Twenty-Five was gone.

"And that would be one for the loss column," Tori said.

"I know," I said, "but there's nothing we can do."

After that experience, Susie's positive reaction to her new gravestone and Colonel Longworth's gracious appreciation on behalf of the whole cemetery population felt especially good.

Back at the shop, Tori bedded down for the night on the sofa, and the cats and I retired to the bedroom to read. After a few minutes, I felt the mattress sag. I looked over the top of my book to find Aunt Fiona sitting at the foot of my bed.

"Well," I said, "there you are."

"Aw, honey," she said, "you didn't really need me."

"So says you," I grumbled. "I could have used a few hints along the way."

"That's why you have Myrtle and Rodney," Aunt Fiona said fondly. "And Tori. I'm thrilled she's going to be running the shop with you."

"You like the coffee shop idea?"

"I love it!" she said. "You and Chase McGregor certainly seem to be getting along."

Studying my aunt's face, I asked, "Are you spying on me?"

Chase and I went to dinner together the night before. At the end of the evening, as he was showing me the beautiful Civil War boots he was making for the Gettysburg film production, he suddenly looked at me and said, "Please don't do anything dangerous like going out to the campground again. I can't stand the thought of anything happening to you."

"You can't?" I said, my voice sounding a breathless.

"No," he said, taking me in his arms, "I can't."

I have mentioned that Chase is a good kisser, right? Like a really, really, *really* good kisser.

When I put the spying question to Aunt Fiona, she huffed up a bit and said, "I prefer the word 'observing.'" She was silent for a moment before adding, "He's a hunk, isn't he?"

Rather than discuss Chase's verifiable hunkiness with my dead aunt, I changed the subject, "Now what do I do?"

"You continue to learn and grow," she smiled. "Make a good life for yourself here in the store."

"Did you have a good life here?" I asked.

"I had a *wonderful* life," she said.

Fumbling with the edge of the quilt, I said, "Am I getting

the witch thing right, Aunt Fiona? I don't want to let you down."

"Oh, honey," she said, "you couldn't possibly let me down. You have the most wonderful heart, Jinx. You always have. That's where being a good witch starts, with a good heart."

"Thank you," I said. "For the store and for my magic and for being you."

Aunt Fiona smiled again. "You're welcome, honey. Now, I have to go. I have people waiting for me."

"There's one more thing I want to know," I said.

"What's that, dear?" Aunt Fiona asked.

"Why couldn't you solve the murders and help the girls?"

My aunt smiled at me. "Because I wasn't as strong as you are, honey," she said. "I could sense the evil, but I didn't have the power of psychometry. I could never have attracted Beth's attention and brought her spirit out of the forest or spoken with the hickory tree the way you did."

"Really?" I said.

"Really," she assured me.

"Will you come back?" I asked hopefully.

"Oh, yes," she said, "I'll pop in from time to time. Now, before I forget, be careful during the shop renovation. Myrtle likes things done a certain way."

"What do you mean a certain . . ."

But Fiona was gone. Seriously, after what we'd just been through, how hard could minor renovation work on the store be?

Note to self. Quit tempting fate with rhetorical questions.

Chapter Thirty-Two

Apartment Above the Cobbler's Shop

"For the love of Bastet, boy," Festus growled. "*Stop* telling people you adopted me at the pound and why in the *hell* is there no whisky in this cream?"

Chase broke four eggs in a bowl and picked up a whisk. "You *look* like a cat from the pound *and* there's no whisky because it's nine o'clock on a Sunday morning."

The yellow cat raised his eyewhiskers. "Your point being what?"

Pausing in mid-whisk, Chase said, "If I have to explain Sunday to you, you're even more of a lost cause than I thought."

"I am aware of the perceived propriety of Sunday," Festus said, stifling a bored yawn.

"Then," Chase said, "you should also be *aware* that I don't want you soused on the one morning of the week we have agreed to eat breakfast together without fail."

Festus flicked his ears in annoyance. "Most people would tell you they like me better when I've had a shot or four. Wakes up my better angels."

Father and son glared at each other for a minute and then they both laughed. "Hard point to argue old man," Chase said, "but I still don't think you need to be swilling Scotch on a Sunday morning—and angels don't drink."

"Any angel looking out after me better drink as a survival tactic," Festus said. "I don't know how in the hell I managed to raise such a stick-in-the-mud self-righteous kid. I don't even remember the last time I darkened the door of a church."

"Fiona's funeral three weeks ago," Chase said, pouring the eggs into a skillet.

"Don't remind me," Festus grumbled. "Fiona's ill-timed demise forced me to spend the day as a biped suffocating in a suit with a silk noose around my neck."

In spite of himself Chase smiled. "They call them *ties*, Dad. Sausage or bacon?"

Festus fixed him with an impassive stare. "That is not an either-or question. Both."

"Which would be why you're getting a gut. You know the vet said you're over your optimal body weight."

"That vet," Festus hissed, narrowing his eyes, "is *below* his optimal mental capacity. I only agreed to be stuffed in a box and taken to that quack because I couldn't stand those damned ear mites. Worst case I've had in years."

"I'm glad you brought that up," Chase said, stirring the eggs. "If you hadn't been hanging out at The Dirty Claw, you wouldn't have caught those ear mites."

Festus flicked his tail lazily back and forth. "If I wanted a nagging wife, I'd get married again. I don't question your social life, boy, so keep your paws off mine."

"Dad . . ."

Using his paw to push the sugar bowl to the edge of the counter, Festus said pleasantly, "Can we get back on topic here or do I have to play hard ball? This stuff is a bitch to sweep up. Gets in every little crack. Attracts ants. Your call, boy."

Chase made an accusatory jab with his wooden spoon. "That's the kind of attitude that gives cats a bad name. This is the same strategy you taught Jinx's cat Winston. It's rude."

"It *works*," Festus said as he nudged the bowl again. "Winston wanted his breakfast on time, and I want mine sans the lectures about my thick fur. You gonna make me do this?"

With a melodramatic sigh, Chase said. "No, I am not. You're not going to ruin my Sunday with your bad manners."

As he watched Chase scoop the eggs into a dish and cover them, the yellow cat said, "Of course I win. I'm older, smarter, and much more handsome than you."

He licked one paw, smoothed back his whiskers, and added, "Those eggs better not be soggy."

With a barely disguised eye roll, Chase said, "You want your eggs cold, because I can arrange that?"

"Now who has an attitude?" Festus asked, eyeing his son with fake innocence.

Choosing to ignore the question, Chase said, "I should have started the meat first, but I was too busy listening to you bitch. If you want to clog your arteries with bacon and sausage, you're going to have to wait. What did you want to talk about anyway?"

"Nice try," Festus said, "but you know perfectly well what I want to talk about—our new resident witch. You know, the one you've got your eye on?"

"I do not have my eye on Jinx. Besides, what's to talk about? She did a great job solving the murders."

Festus jumped from the counter to the table. "There are protocols for this kind of thing. No one warned us a new witch was coming online. If I can't have whisky, can I get some coffee in this cream?"

Chase moved to the table with the coffee pot. "Be fair, Dad. Fiona didn't know Jinx would put in a post-mortem request to inherit powers. Fiona's ghost popped over and told us as soon as she could."

Lowering his head to lap at the coffee bowl, Festus grumbled, "Kathleen would have known in advance. She respected our role as the protectors of the Daughters of Knasgowa."

Looking down at his father, Chase said, "You still miss her, don't you?"

Still drinking his coffee, Festus said, "I will always miss her. Kelly, too."

"Kelly isn't dead."

At that, the old cat sat back and directed his attention out the window. "A part of her is dead. She's turned her back on her magic and raised her daughter in total ignorance of her heritage."

For a few seconds nothing but the sizzle of the cooking bacon broke the silence. "Kelly had her reasons for abandoning magic," Chase said softly. "She was afraid that if she followed in Kathleen's footsteps, she would put Jinx in danger."

Still watching the courthouse square, Festus asked, "Allowing the line to be broken, suppressing Jinx's powers, and pushing all of us away was not the way to ensure Jinx's safety."

Chase carried their food to the table and sat down. "Kathleen and Mo did the best they could to engineer a work around. Mo taught Tori about mountain magic, so she could be ready when Jinx received her magic."

When Chase picked up his fork, Festus slapped him hard across the knuckles.

"Ouch!" Chase yelped. "You had your claws out. What the *hell*, Dad?"

"Remember?" Festus said sweetly. "It's Sunday. Be reverent, boy. Say grace."

Rubbing the four red welts across his hand, Chase lowered his head, "Thank you for this food and bless it to the nourishment of our bodies. Amen."

"Amen," Festus intoned with faux solemnity. "Now, what were we talking about?"

Flexing his fingers, Chase retrieved his fork. "I was saying that Tori has handled everything beautifully so far. She supported Jinx. She wasn't rattled about the magic or the ghosts. They're going to be a great team. Plus, there's every reason to believe Jinx will have abilities equal to her mother's in time."

Festus looked down at his plate. "Yeah, yeah. Gemma's kid is doing her job. Did you have to be so damned stingy with the bacon?"

"I don't enjoy being chewed out by the vet about your weight," Chase said. "There's no reason to get all upset about protocols. We may not have had any warning that Jinx would take up her powers, but she's even exceeded Myrtle's expectations. Psychometry is an advanced skill."

"Which," Festus said, biting into his bacon, "would be why you don't give a baby witch a loaded wand. Jinx is a long way from being up to speed."

"You can't know that," Chase protested. "Besides, Myrtle will help her."

"Jinx thinks *Myrtle* is nothing but a cute magical inventory clerk."

"Myrtle knows what she's doing," Chase said defensively. "Jinx can't handle a full information dump right now. Show some empathy, Dad."

Licking butter off his toast, Festus said, "Son, we need to have a serious conversation about this. You can't let yourself develop feelings for Jinx. You know that's against the rules."

"Says the werecat who routinely gets the woman to rub his ears."

Festus chuckled. "I can't wait to see the look on her face when she finds out the truth about me."

"You are awful."

"It's part of my charm," Festus said, before belching loudly.

"Nice table manners, Dad, real nice."

The yellow cat grew serious again. "Look, son, I've been doing this a long time. Working with Kathleen and Rebecca spoiled me. I liked Fiona, but she wasn't the next in line for a reason. At best her powers were erratic."

Chase leaned back. "What was it like for Kathleen when Rebecca died?"

A sad, faraway look came into the cat's amber eyes. "There are meant to be two," he said softly. "Kathleen survived. She was too strong not to, but losing Padric and then her best friend? The loneliness almost killed her. Thank God nothing serious happened during those years."

"Maybe things will stay quiet for Jinx, too," Chase said, absently shoving the food around on his plate.

"I know you'd like that, son," Festus said. "You want to lead a normal human life, but you have to accept it, Chase. We are not human. Even if the spell on Knasgowa's grave holds, Chesterfield is still out there."

"Don't buy trouble," Chase said irritably. "Let Jinx enjoy this. She has plans for the store. She's already managed to use her magic to do something good. Things could stay quiet for years."

Giving his plate a final lick, Festus patted his paw on the coffee bowl. Chase topped it off and added more cream.

They sat in silence until Festus cleared his throat.

"If you've got to toss a hairball, get off the table," Chase warned.

"I'm not going to toss a hairball," Festus said irritably. "I'm trying to get you to listen to me. Surely, you can sense the untapped potential of Jinx's powers."

"I can."

"I'm not arguing that the kid has gotten off to a great start.

Giving Jane Doe her name and catching a murderer with psychometry is impressive. Kathleen would be proud."

Chase met his father's eyes. "Then what's your problem?"

"A son who doesn't seem to remember that magic has a life of its own," Festus countered. "Jinx pulled the cork out of the bottle when she asked for her powers. She has no clue how to tamp down abilities that have been simmering in the background for almost thirty years. She will make a mistake, Chase, probably a big one. She needs to know that she isn't alone."

"Not our call, Dad. You've already put your case to Myrtle, and she said no. For now, I'm the helpful cobbler next door, and you're my adopted, lame cat from the pound."

Festus' ears went flat. "You're both going to be sorry you didn't listen to me. Somebody should be keeping a closer eye on Jinx."

"Fine," Chase said. "Work with her cats. You've already been sneaking over there through the crawl space and gossiping with them."

"Cats," Festus said with pointed emphasis, "do not gossip, which you would know if you didn't waste the majority of your time going around on two legs. Felines *exchange information*."

Chase held up his hands. "My bad. Continue to *exchange information* with her cats if it makes you feel better. But I'm telling you, Jinx has a cautious nature. She's not going to do anything stupid."

"You want to put your money where your mouth is?" Festus asked, with a gleam in his eye.

"Sure."

Festus thought for a minute. "Jinx doesn't screw up, I eat the way the vet wants me to."

"And if she does screw up?" Chase asked, with a wary look in his eye.

"I get whisky in my Sunday coffee for a month with no old

lady lectures from you." He licked his paw and held it out to his son. "Deal?"

Chase rolled his eyes again. "Do we have to do the spit handshake?"

"We do."

"Okay, fine," Chase said, spitting and shaking his father's hand. "But you just made a sucker bet."

Festus drew his whiskers back in a Cheshire cat grin. "I damn sure did," he said, "and the sucker would be you. Now, if you'll excuse me, I have a date with a sun puddle."

With that, he jumped off the table and started down the stairs, calling back over his shoulder, "Oh, and do something about my box, would you?"

"Sure, Dad," Chase said sarcastically, "anything else I can do for you?"

"Yeah," Festus said, his voice growing fainter as he descended. "When I win that bet, I want the good stuff. Oban. And none of that 14-year-old crap. Buy the twenty-one."

"That's $500 a bottle," Chase protested.

With a final flounce of his tail, Festus said, "Five-hundred and eighty-nine. But what's money between a father and his son?"

Padding across the empty cobbler shop, Festus stood on his hind legs, turned the key in the lock, nudged the door open with his head, and limped out to his bench. Settling into a warm, glorious pool of sunlight, he closed his eyes.

"Damn," he thought as he drifted off to sleep, *"that creamed whisky is gonna taste good."*

A Word from Juliette

Thank you for reading *Witch at Heart*. Now that you've reached the end of the book, I hope you'll want to continue the adventure with Jinx, Tori, and the gang in Briar Hollow and beyond.

The story develops through a page-turning series of urban fantasy novels that take the characters into new adventures and realms.

The next story, *Witch at Odds*, puts Jinx in the awkward position of learning the consequence of getting too brave with her magic, too soon.

Not certain you want to continue the journey? I've included the first chapter of *Witch at Odds* to give you a sneak peak of the mystery, adventure, and hijinks lying ahead!

But first . . . Get Exclusive Jinx Hamilton Material

There are many things I love about being an author, but building a relationship with my readers is far and away the best.

Once a month I send out a newsletter with information on new releases, sneak peeks, and inside articles on Jinx Hamilton as well as other books and series I'm currently developing.

You can get all this and more by signing up here.

Witch at Odds - Preview

"What could go wrong?"

Let's begin with those famous last words, shall we?

This whole thing started when I decided to add a room onto the back of the store I inherited from Aunt Fiona. Okay, that and a few *simple* renovations to implement a great idea for a coffee shop/espresso bar.

My first mistake was in forgetting to run the plans by the store itself for her approval.

Yeah, you read that right.

My store is . . . well, I don't know what my store is, but her name is Myrtle.

Not to be all anthropomorphic or anything, but she's very much a "person."

In the short time I've been in residence, Myrtle has never been anything but helpful. She quietly leads me, on request, to things I'd never be able to find on my own in the hopeless jumble that passes for inventory.

She actually has a good sense of humor and something of

a maternal streak. Of course, when I was thickheaded about something early in our relationship, Myrtle did whiz an arrow past my nose, but my own mother threw a knife at me once.

(Okay, *fine*, in case my mother ever reads this, she claims her hands were wet and the knife slipped. All I know is that a sharp piece of cutlery landed at my feet. I quit arguing and did as I was told. Myrtle achieved much the same reaction from me with her arrow.)

I should have known Myrtle would prefer to have things done her way, mainly because my deceased Aunt Fiona warned me about it. Yes, Aunt Fiona still pops in from time to time. There's no reason death *has* to be a self-limiting experience. For heaven's sake, think outside the box (or the casket as the case may be.)

So, long about now, you're probably wondering if I'm completely nuts. Probably, but I'm also a witch. That was Aunt Fiona's other bequest to me—magical powers. The fact that I'm a newly minted witch goes a long way toward explaining the story I'm about to tell you.

But, first, let's briefly backtrack. Hi, my name is Jinx Hamilton. My business sits on the Briar Hollow courthouse square between Chase McGregor's cobbler shop and Amity Prescott's art gallery.

Chase is on the fast track to becoming my boyfriend, and Amity is flaky, creative, and anxious for us to do some joint functions once my coffee shop is up and running.

Then there's Tori, whose official title in my life is BFF. She's also my brand-new business partner, the fulfillment of a plan we hatched when we were six and set up our first lemonade stand.

Tori quit her job at Tom's Cafe and will move into the room out back once it's finished. It was her idea to do both construction projects at one time, so technically this was all her fault. (That's my story, and I'm sticking to it.)

The paint gave us the first hint we might be in for trouble. Walking in the store's front door amounts to entering a time warp. Think antique display cabinets, beautifully worn wood floors, and an old, elegant tin ceiling. The walls were a sort of indistinct stucco tannish, white *thing*.

Tori thought some color in the coffee area would help give the place a "funky, bohemian vibe." We're hoping to bring in local musicians on the weekends, and maybe even serve beer and wine if my license application goes through. The whole planned decorating scheme felt right, so I was on board.

Tori drove over to one of the big box hardware places and picked up a variety of paint samples. The palette ran the gamut from aubergine to chartreuse, but no matter what color she put on the wall, Myrtle instantly turned it to aged tan.

It was all I could do not to laugh, which would have infuriated Tori and encouraged Myrtle.

Tori stood there with her dripping fuchsia paintbrush and glared at the store, which meant her head was on a swivel since we don't exactly know where to look when we talk to Myrtle.

"Knock it off, Myrtle," Tori demanded. "Don't you want to *live* a little?"

Since Myrtle instantly blew Tori a raspberry, we'll assume the answer was "no."

As diplomatically as I could manage since Tori can be. . . *firm-minded*, I said, "I don't think it's a good idea to annoy the building we're living in. Why don't we go for funky retro bohemian and keep the . . . uh . . . current, tasteful vintage appeal?"

Still brandishing her paintbrush, Tori wheeled on me and said accusingly, "Suck-up."

"I'm good with that," I said earnestly, "totally."

We abandoned the painting plan for the moment, which I hoped Myrtle would see as a show of support, or even out and out obedience. As I was about to find out, however, the dispute was far from over.

The next day, Mark the contractor's guys started trying to relocate the floor-to-ceiling wooden cases currently occupying the corner between the staircase and the east wall. We needed the extra space for the coffee bar.

Tori was nowhere to be seen. Earlier in the day, she ran a few errands and then excused herself to continue her research into proper espresso preparation. That was a fairly adult way to say that she was still ticked off about yesterday and was, frankly, pouting.

Now, understand, I would never actually use the word "pout" with her, but as my mother would so eloquently put it, if Tori's lower lip pushed out any further, she would've tripped over it.

I felt vaguely like a kindergarten teacher attempting to forestall a playground riot.

As the men started to move the cabinets, I was the only official witness to what happened next, which was a lot of nothing.

After an impressive amount of grunting, groaning, and suppressed swearing, Mark stood back, scratched his head in obvious puzzlement and said, "The dang things won't budge. Looks like we're going to have to take a crowbar to this situation. It's a shame because we'll probably destroy the cabinets, but I don't know what else to do."

When he used the word "destroy," Myrtle let out a menacing rattle.

"What the heck was that?" Mark asked, looking around with alarm.

"Air in the pipes," I lied smoothly.

"Maybe we need to get a plumber in here," he said with concern. "The last thing you want is a flood."

"No, no," I said. "We're good. Give us the night to think about the display cases. We'll talk about it tomorrow. Okay?"

As soon as he was gone, I put my hands on my hips and said, "Okay, Myrtle, you and I have to talk about this situation *now*."

Even I have a hard time taking myself seriously when I'm speaking to thin air, which is why these conversations only happen when the store is empty. If anyone witnessed one of my exchanges with Myrtle, I'd be fitted for a snug jacket with really, really long sleeves.

"Myrtle, look," I said, "I'm sorry. I should have talked to you about our plans before the work started. We're not trying to do anything to hurt you."

Then it dawned on me.

Did the renovations cause Myrtle actual *pain*?

"Oh my God, Myrtle," I said, a note of panic coming into my voice. "Are we hurting you?"

To my immense relief, the rack of Briar Hollow souvenir sun visors by the counter bobbled back and forth in the recognized sign for "no."

"Ok, good," I said. "We don't want to hurt you, but we need you to be less set in your ways. Everything changes, Myrtle, including interior decorating schemes."

Myrtle answered with a long, drawn-out exhalation. She sounded wearily patient.

"Fine, I'll give you that one," I admitted. "We don't really *have* a decorating scheme. The whole eclectic thing worked for Aunt Fiona. She kept this place going because she was such a character. I'm more ordinary than that, which you apparently like, but Tori isn't ordinary at all."

Case in point. Right now, the ends of my BFF's short, spiky, blond hair are a glowing shade of magenta.

"Tori is going to be living with us," I continued. "She is part of the family. She *will* come up with crazy ideas. It's who she is. Come on, Myrtle. You lived with Aunt Fiona for years. How can you not be used to crazy?"

Out of nowhere a Polaroid picture of my aunt fluttered down and landed at my feet. I picked up the snapshot and studied it. That was Aunt Fiona alright. Although she was smiling into the camera with her usual impish expression, the rest of her was remarkably bland. My aunt was wearing what my mother derisively referred to as her “winter uniform.” A gray sweatshirt, baggy jeans, and running shoes.

"Are you trying to tell me that Tori is too colorful for you in the actual sense of *color*?” I asked Myrtle.

A small shower of gold stars fluttered down around me, the kind that teachers give children who cut straight lines with their blunt-nosed scissors.

"Okay,” I said, ignoring Myrtle’s obvious condescension, "how about we compromise. I'll get her to tone down the color if you'll relax and not be worried about us moving a few things around.”

Myrtle answered with a hum that indicated she was thinking about it. I decided to press my slim advantage with more groveling.

“I know I should have asked your opinion, and I will from now on, but will you please let the guys move the display cases in the morning? They’re just going right over there,” I said, pointing.

A drawer in one of the cases slid open with remarkable defiance, releasing a paintbrush that floated briskly in front of my face and snapped neatly in two. I couldn’t help myself; I laughed.

“I get it; I get it,” I said. “No painting. But are we good to go on the work to put in the coffee bar? It’s just a sink, a work surface, a fridge, and a counter—and there will be some tables right in here.” Again, I gestured with my arms.

After a minute, the sun visors nodded.

“Thank you,” I said.

I felt like a diplomat who avoided a missile launch.

Now for phase two. I had to go upstairs and deal with the other half of the standoff—my BFF who was no doubt sulking on the couch with the cats.

Color me right. That's exactly where I found Tori, but she was *not* in her happy place.

Now, my cats, Zeke, Yule, Xavier, and Winston looked like they were having the time of their lives—the comatose time of their lives. All concerned were snoring.

"Hi," I said, claiming the big easy chair. "Myrtle and I had a summit conference. We're good to go on moving the cabinets, but it's thumbs down on the painting still."

"Harrumph," Tori grumbled, scratching Zeke's ears and staring at the TV.

Covering my eyes with my hand and shaking my head, I said, "Seriously, Tori, I think you're outgunned this time. Is going to war with a magical building really the battle you want to pick?"

Tori grabbed one of the sofa pillows and held it defensively against her chest—the same way she used to clutch her teddy bear, Rufus, when we were kids. "I guess not," she admitted glumly. "But my color scheme rocked."

"It did," I said soothingly. "There was rockage. You can use any color you want in your own room."

"I didn't expect Myrtle to act so freaking *old*," Tori grumbled.

Since this did not seem to be the time to point out that we hadn't expected the store to do anything but sit there and be a building, I opted for Plan B: red wine, popcorn, and repeat binge-watching the last season of *Scandal*.

By three episodes in, Tori was far more interested in debating the merits of Team Jake v. Team Fitz than she was in Myrtle's frame of mind.

(For the record, I have *so* had enough of Fitz. Dude, just run the country already.)

Sometime around eleven, I looked over to see that Tori had joined the feline snooze-fest. I quietly turned off the TV, threw a blanket over her and the cats, and carried my laptop into the bedroom.

Time for class.

Also by Juliette Harper

In the Jinx Hamilton Series:

ALL Books Available in KindleUnlimited!

Witch at Odds

Jinx accepts her new life as a witch and is determined to make a success of both that and her new business. However, she has a great deal to learn. As the story unfolds, Jinx sets out to both study her craft and to get a real direction for her aunt's haphazard approach to inventory. Although Jinx can call on Aunt Fiona's ghost for help, the old lady is far too busy living a jet set afterlife to be worried about her niece's learning curve. That sets Jinx up to make a major mistake and to figure out how to set things right again.

Buy Witch at Odds

In the Jinx Hamilton/ Wrecking Crew Novellas:

Moonstone

Werecat Festus McGregor leads his Recovery of Magical Objects Squad on a mission to retrieve the Moonstone Spoon from the penthouse of eccentric financier and collector Wardlaw Magwilde. Festus has the operation planned to the last detail until a wereparrot and a member of his own team throw a monkey wrench in the works -- but thankfully no actual monkeys.

Join Festus, Rube and the rest of the raccoons in this fun-filled novella from the bestselling author of the Jinx Hamilton series. Filled with hysterical Fae acronyms and overlapping agency jurisdictions, Moonstone is an escapist romp you won't want to put down.

Buy Moonstone

Merstone

A werecat and a raccoon walk into a dragon's lair . . .

Join ROMO agent and werecat Festus McGregor in this second installment of the Jinx Hamilton/ Wrecking Crew novellas. Agreeing to an off-the-books mission with wereparrot Jilly Pepperdine, Festus and Rube find themselves on the Isle of Wight in search of an ancient lodestone with the power to enslave shifters.

The perfect match of whimsical fun and fantastical adventure, enjoy the latest novella from bestselling author Juliette Harper. An escapist romp in the Fae world where magic, artifacts, and laughter abound!

Buy Merstone

The Selby Jensen Paranormal Mysteries

Descendants of the Rose

Selby Jensen's business card reads "Private Investigator," but that seriously downplays her occupation. Let's hear it in her own words:

"You want to know what I do for a living? I rip souls out. Cut heads off. Put silver bullets where silver bullets need putting. You think there aren't any monsters? . . . I have some disturbing news for you. You might want to sit down. Monsters walk among us. I'm looking for one in particular. In the meantime? I'm keeping the rest of them from eating people like you."

Juliette Harper, author of The Jinx Hamilton Novels, creates a cast of characters, most of whom have one thing in common; they don't have a pulse. The dead are doing just fine by Selby, who is determined never to lose someone she loves again, but then a force of love more powerful than her grief changes that plan.

Join Selby Jensen as she and her team track down a shadowy figure tied to a murder at a girls' school. What none of them realize, however, is that in solving this case, they will enter a longer battle against a larger evil.

Buy Descendants of the Rose

The Study Club Mysteries

You Can't Get Blood Out of Shag Carpet

Wanda Jean Milton discovers her husband, local exterminator Hilton Milton, dead on her new shag carpet with an Old Hickory carving knife sticking out of his chest.

Beside herself over how she'll remove the stain, and grief-stricken over Hilton's demise, Wanda Jean finds herself the prime suspect. But she is also a member of "the" local Study Club, a bastion of independent Texas feminism 1960s style.

Club President Clara Wyler has no intention of allowing a member to be a murder suspect. Aided by her younger sister and County Clerk, Mae Ella Gormley; Sugar Watson, the proprietress of Sugar's Style and Spray; and Wilma Schneider, Army MASH veteran and local RN, the Club women set out to clear Wanda Jean's name — never guessing the local dirt they'll uncover.

Buy You Can't Get Blood Out of Shag Carpet

About the Author

"It's kind of fun to do the impossible." Walt Disney said that, and the two halves of Juliette Harper believe it wholeheartedly. Together, Massachusetts-based Patricia Pauletti, and Texan Rana K. Williamson combine their writing talents as Juliette. "She" loves to create strong female characters and place them in interesting, challenging, painful, and often comical situations. Refusing to be bound by genre, Juliette's primary interest lies in telling good stories. Patti, who fell in love with writing when she won her first 8th grade poetry contest, has a background in music, with a love of art and design. Rana, a former journalist and university history instructor, is happiest with a camera in hand and a cat or two at home.

For more information . . .
www.JulietteHarper.com
admin@julietteharper.com

By Juliette Harper

Skye House Publishing, LLC

This is a work of fiction. Names, characters, businesses, places, events, and incidents are either the products of the author's imagination or used in a fictitious manner. Any resemblance to actual persons, living or dead, or actual events is purely coincidental.

EBOOK ISBN: 978-1-943516-84-1

PRINT ISBN: 978-1-943516-85-8

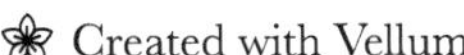

Printed in Great Britain
by Amazon